NaGeira

"Butler's prose is smooth and clean; the story moves forward vigorously, with patches of poetry."
THE GLOBE AND MAIL

"Butler keeps the story grounded, brisk and inviting."
THE TELEGRAM

"A tour de force of the imagination . . ."
CANADIAN BOOK REVIEW ANNUAL

"[A] brilliant exploration of one of Newfoundland's central mythological figures set within highly-crafted, well-written parallel stories that hinge on twists of fate and an intricate plot structure."
ATLANTIC BOOKS TODAY

Stoker's Shadow

"Butler's prose style is often lush—he describes post-Victorian London quite eloquently . . ."
THE GLOBE AND MAIL

"Though the vampires in Bram Stoker's novel *Dracula* cast no shadows, the author and the book certainly do. In *Stoker's Shadow*, Paul Butler explores this phenomenon in a unique blending of biography and dreamscape."
DR. ELIZABETH MILLER

"*Stoker's Shadow* is an interesting read because of its unique approach and its historical insights."
THE HERALD

TITANIC ASHES

A NOVEL

TITANIC ASHES

A NOVEL

PAUL BUTLER

PENNYWELL BOOKS
ST. JOHN'S

Library and Archives Canada Cataloguing in Publication

Butler, Paul, 1964-
Titanic ashes / Paul Butler.

Issued also in electronic format.
ISBN 978-1-926881-52-2

1. Titanic (Steamship)--Fiction. I. Title.

PS8553.U735T58 2012   C813'.6   C2011-906524-X

© 2012 by Paul Butler

ALL RIGHTS RESERVED. No part of the work covered by the copyright hereon may be reproduced or used in any form or by any means—graphic, electronic or mechanical—without the written permission of the publisher. Any request for photocopying, recording, taping or information storage and retrieval systems of any part of this book shall be directed to Access Copyright, The Canadian Copyright Licensing Agency, 1 Yonge Street, Suite 800, Toronto, ON M5E 1E5. This applies to classroom use as well.

PRINTED IN CANADA

This paper has been certified to meet the environmental and social standards of the Forest Stewardship Council® (FSC®) and comes from responsibly managed forests, and verified recycled sources.

Cover Design: Adam Freake   Edited by Marnie Parsons and Annamarie Beckel

PENNYWELL BOOKS IS AN IMPRINT OF FLANKER PRESS LIMITED.

—— Flanker Press Limited ——
PO Box 2522, Station C St. John's, NL Canada
Toll Free: 1-866-739-4420 www.flankerpress.com

16 15 14 13 12   1 2 3 4 5 6 7 8

 Canada Council   Conseil des Arts
for the Arts   du Canada

We acknowledge the financial support of the Government of Canada through the Book Publishing Industry Development Program (BPIDP) for our publishing activities; the Canada Council for the Arts which last year invested $24.3 million in writing and publishing throughout Canada; the Government of Newfoundland and Labrador, Department of Tourism, Culture and Recreation.

For my parents,
Anne Frances and John Frederick

chapter one

EVEN THROUGH THE STAR-SHAPED gap in the foliage, Mr. Ismay's face is unmistakable. Dark eyes glisten like those of a man freshly wounded; his brow furrows; his mouth hides behind a grey moustache. Miranda peers through the leafy opening, feeling protected for the moment, the way an audience member feels shielded by the relative darkness of the stalls and the sense of invisibility. But this is a restaurant, she reminds herself, not a theatre. He could turn to her any time, and no doubt will, if she doesn't tear her own gaze away.

Her mother has been talking about curtains, how the modern vogue for sheer makes her think she is entering a harem. This is rich, Miranda thinks. Clinging to the late Victorian fashions of her girlhood, Mother insists on mauve and indigo drapes in her own home, surely the signature hues of ill-repute.

It is, in any case, a ruse. Mother is merely trying to

probe into Miranda's plans, but she's trying too hard, using a barrage of noise when a simple question might yield more information. Mother wants to know where Graham and she will buy and how she intends to decorate her first marital home.

Married life is Miranda's escape, and Graham is under strict orders to keep mum. She wants to preserve at least the pretence that everything will be quite different, unsullied by parental influence. But Graham is a chivalrous man and his expression becomes more desperate each time he is compelled to give an evasive answer.

It was the *clink* of ice within a water jug that made Miranda turn to an adjacent table a few moments ago. Her gaze moved into the middle distance, and then beyond, where an image claimed her attention. Through the star-shaped gap, cigar smoke parted like the haze one sees around the subject of an old portrait photograph. He had paused, soup spoon halfway toward his mouth, listening to someone with an interest that seemed not quite sincere. He nodded, crinkled his eyes and gave an upward twitch of his moustache—as though reacting to a funny story—then took his food and chewed.

Miranda suspected it was him straightaway. She knew from experience that only when one is most desperate to be mistaken, only then does one's first instinct turn out to be spot on. The floor tipped beneath her. She held the cool stem of her champagne flute and felt perspiration from her fingertips mingle with condensation from the glass.

Before she saw him she was wishing her mother would shut up. Now she is glad for the incessant stream of words. It means no one will notice the change in her. Poor Graham nods inexhaustibly and even tries the occasional interjection, only to agree of course. Father is off somewhere else, cutting grimly with his knife as though searching for his cutlet's most profitable seam.

"You are so lucky, you two," Mother continues, "beginning your young lives in London." She gazes regretfully at her husband who, deserting his meat for the moment, begins to forage through his cabbage. "For our first several years of married life we were stuck in the provinces. And you will be ensconced here from the very start!" A sparkle in the eyes now, a promise to her soon-to-be son-in-law about the wonders that await him; the irritation is enough to make Miranda forget her panic.

"Mother, Graham has lived and worked in London for more than five years. London isn't adventure to him, or to me. It's just life." She keeps her voice low. The last thing she wants is to draw attention to her table.

"Life changes when one marries, Miranda dear. The world opens up."

The phrase sends a new terror through her, and she wishes she hadn't spoken. Reminiscences of transatlantic voyages are now only two or three exchanges away. A quick glance through the palm shows Mr. Ismay's face more clearly than before. All he has to do is turn his head and she, and possibly her whole table, will be easily visible to him.

"And will you be travelling to America with your new bride, Graham dear?"

The subject opens even sooner than she thought. The table seems to rock gently.

Graham coughs. This is the first real question, the first at any rate to be followed by a pause long enough for answering, but unfortunately—or perhaps fortunately—Graham has chosen this moment to take a bite of his wood pigeon. He chews quickly and brings his napkin to his lips.

Miranda steals another glance through the leaves. Mr. Ismay's face is out of sight for the moment, the dome of his balding head bobbing toward the table.

"We thought closer to home at first," says Graham. "Honeymoon in Paris, that kind of thing."

"Oh yes, I know about that, but afterwards? This is the age of speed. America is the new Europe, you know, Graham dear. In a year or two of married life you'll be simply yearning for adventure."

Mother takes a rather sly look at Father, who reaches for a tumbler of water. She won't leave the subject alone now. The one escape for Miranda is to excuse herself for a few minutes, but this might be dangerous. Mr. Ismay might remain unaware of her all evening if she stays in her seat, but any movement might catch his eye. And, curious or not, his eyes would then likely follow her back to the table. Even if he doesn't recognize Miranda, he would surely remember her parents.

"Of course adventure is in my blood. My father was a shipbuilder in Halifax, Nova Scotia, and there was always romance in our family. I've tried my best to pass it on." Miranda hears a note of regret as Mother looks at her wistfully. "We spent a glorious summer in New York when Miranda was just ten years old. Do you remember, dear?"

"Yes, Mother. I remember." She weighs the words carefully. If her mother were in a mood to notice she might pick up on the undercurrent of warning, but Miranda knows this is too hopeful. Mother is immune to any such sirens.

In real terms, her mother should have more reason to avoid the subject of the "glorious summer in New York" than she, but it never seems to work out that way. While immune to the emotion herself, Agnes Grimsden marshals the threat of embarrassment with psychological insight and ruthless efficiency. She knows Miranda is more afraid of the subject than she, and there's nothing Miranda can do to change this fact.

"And there was that dreadful, tragic event from which we all had to recover first," Mother says. "Well, I'm sure Miranda must have told you, though I know she doesn't like to talk about it."

Miranda wonders what she must look like. Part of her skin is overtaken with a shivery coolness, part is blushing. She imagines a patchwork of white and red, and shrinks into herself, certain her reptilian appearance will draw attention from everyone in the restaurant, including the man beyond the palm.

She meets Graham's gaze for the first time in ten minutes, and only furtively. His grey eyes waver with a mixture of sympathy and muted curiosity. She has told him about the *Titanic*, of course, and alluded to doing something in the aftermath of which she was ashamed. She has hinted, also, of other troubles, not so much of her own making, but still tangled up with her shame. It has all been done with the mildest hints. Graham has that rather wonderful, rare quality of picking up on nuance, silence, and discomfort. He respects and keeps clear of tender spots in Miranda's memory. Miranda has told him next to nothing. But it is enough, and in any case the suggestion of a taboo is overshadowed by the event which preceded it all. Silence must seem fairly reasonable in the circumstances.

What she saw, experienced, and how she reacted in delayed panic, is locked away tight and will likely remain so. Sensitive, respectful Graham knows not to delve or prod. Mother, however, is not like Graham. Even if she accepted the notion of a taboo, she would go blustering through it.

"No," says Graham quietly, his eyes moving from Miranda to Mother. "She doesn't like to talk about it."

"Such an experience, so many lives lost!"

"Indeed." Graham coughs as though nudging toward a change in subject.

"Miranda's father wasn't travelling with us," says Mother, as if her husband weren't present at the table. "Thank goodness, because John is noble and selfless. He would have insisted on remaining behind on the ship, and we would have been left destitute."

Father coughs, his frown tightening as he takes another sip of water.

"If you'll forgive me, Mother." Miranda is unable to contain herself. "The logic of that statement somewhat eludes me. A selfless act surely doesn't leave a man's family destitute."

"Honour, my dear," Mother says, raising her glass in a dark parody of a toast. "An old concept, I admit, but an important one nonetheless." There is harshness in her expression now.

Perhaps she and Graham have gone too far in stonewalling about their intended home, its location and décor. People like Mother, who dominate conversations, are like that sometimes. They take a long time to feel offence, even to notice the lack of response, but once they have taken umbrage, it's too late; by that time they've given too much of themselves, and they feel foolish and shunned. Was it mean of her to say nothing to Mother about the curtains, not to ask her advice about something inconsequential? Was it meaner still to draw genial Graham into being her proxy, to insist he brush her off too?

"Well," Miranda says, her face burning. "Thank goodness Father was never put in the position of deciding what he must do."

Father grunts and takes another sip of water, leaning back in his chair and looking from one face to another. Miranda wonders how they have managed to arrive at this point in the conversation. All she has wanted to do since glimpsing the face through the palms is to keep the talk away from the subject of travel by sea in general, transatlantic liners in particular, and, in minute particular, the *Titanic* and the disaster of 1912. And here they are, not only discussing the *Titanic* but the very heart of Miranda's current anxiety: notions of valour and cowardice as they pertain to gentlemen going down with the ship or stepping into lifeboats.

"You would have insisted upon staying aboard the doomed liner, would you not have, John?" her mother asks.

Father lets his fingers dip absentmindedly into his waistcoat pocket as though checking for a watch. "Indubitably," he says with a slight sniff and quick glance around at the company.

Not many people understand Father's sense of humour,

but Miranda does. Buried beneath the gruff exterior is a subtle and many-layered malice that lends the simplest of gestures, the most straightforward-seeming of statements, a contrary meaning. Mother is satisfied and gives Miranda a cool nod of victory. But Miranda knows Father's one-word answer refers not to honour but merely to the fact he would have preferred to be free of his wife then and there, even if death were the only option of escape. Mother's extroversion saves her from this knowledge. She simply isn't able to hide an emotion once it surfaces, and can't fathom people who can.

But while Father can obscure true meanings from his wife, Miranda sees little chance of hiding anything. She wanted to protect herself from any conversation of transatlantic liners, and failed. She wanted to keep off the subject of the *Titanic*, and failed. Already Mother has peeled the subject down to the sore points of lifeboats and honour. Only one creaking gate remains unbreached: J. Bruce Ismay, White Star Line Chairman, and Director of the International Mercantile Marine Company, one-time acquaintance of Miranda's parents—and the man sitting beyond the palm.

"In any case, Miranda dear, you were not always so disparaging to the traditional virtues of courage and chivalry," Mother says, luxuriating in the moment, like the soft breeze that touches the palm's heart-shaped leaves and sets them quivering.

"Nor am I now, Mother." Miranda's reply, firm and final, seems to take the wind out of her mother's sails. Her expression drops, and her eyes cease to smile; she takes a glance at her husband and then at Graham, as though suddenly worried she has been caught misbehaving.

"Oh look," says Graham, "the band is back."

With some relief, Miranda cranes her neck half circle toward the dais, which is partially shrouded on both sides by rather extravagant greenery, so that when the musicians take up their instruments it looks as if they have just stepped out from a jungle into a clearing to find the means of entertainment miraculously awaiting them. They take position and briefly strike some notes to make sure they are still in tune. The violinist nods to the bass player. The cellist readies his bow before the strings, and with a sweet high yap the quartet swings into a ragtime number. A collective gasp of pleasure breathes through the diners, and insulated by waves of sound and a single focus for their attention, Miranda breathes more easily. Mother, apparently forgetting the unpleasant undercurrents of the conversation, taps her fingers gaily and her smile takes in everyone at the table, including Miranda.

chapter two

EVELYN LOOKS ACROSS AT Father, at his troubled moustache and chalky skin. The joke she attempted was one of Basil's. Had it worked, had Father's eyes not been glassy and preoccupied, had his head not bobbed mechanically back toward his dinner, she would have told him the source. She wants to talk about Basil, feels the subject ought to bring him back to himself. He should be glad. His daughter is stepping out with a man who, like his own younger self, is a shipping agent; who, also like himself, will be the likely inheritor of chairmanships and directorships. He couldn't wish for greater proof of her pride in him, could he?

Evelyn's mother tries so hard to reassure him of her feelings and her respect. But there is so little she can do to prove this that would be in any way dynamic enough to capture his attention. She can't remarry Father without divorcing him first. But his daughters can make it quite clear they think their mother chose well if they make similar choices themselves. In marrying Basil Sanderson, Evelyn will quite literally be bringing the White Star Line back into the family.

But it might be just as well to leave the subject for tonight. Basil—Shipping—Father—*Titanic*. It's all too close. She saw the Grimsdens a few minutes ago. Ever since, she has felt breathless and unsteady. It's as though she is leading poor Father along a high wire, a silent crowd beneath watching for the one slip that will bring them hurtling to disaster. If she mentioned Basil, Father would think not of his own career, but of one terrible night. He would think of Basil not as a shipping agent, or director, or son of his own colleague and friend, but as a war hero. He might focus on that term *hero*, and its opposite, a painful word, used over and over to describe himself. Tonight, it seems, all words are laying traps.

"That must be one of Basil's," says Father unexpectedly, just as Evelyn thought he had drifted off. There is a vague, tired smile on his face. He seems like a man who has floated from the earth and is trying to find his way back through layers of haze and mist.

"Yes, Father."

"And how is he?"

"Fine, Father, in fine form."

Father gives another faraway smile and his head nods once more toward his plate.

The *Titanic* is with them, and has been haunting Evelyn even before she was conscious of the Grimsdens' presence. She thought at first it was because she was with her father in this leafy, extravagant restaurant, breezy and luxurious in the way the great ocean liners must have been before the war. A band swirled through popular tunes, some modern, and some—like "Daisy, Daisy," which greeted her entrance—reaching back to that bygone era for which the older patrons no doubt yearn. The place oozes with the unapologetic pre-war opulence that has long since gone underground, except in places like this. Everything these days is sleek, clear lines. Rampant foliage, and ornate mirrors, and lights are bound to haul one back to an earlier time.

Although Father took that fateful voyage alone, it never feels that way. And the experience—pieced together through fragments of first-hand accounts, imagination and daydreams, as well as from the constant heightened empathy she feels with her father—have been especially strong since she stepped into the Palm Room on her father's arm. She sensed the *Titanic* in a chill around her shoulders, in objects just beyond her field of vision, the curl of a moustache or the wave of a fan. She heard it in the discordant swell of conversation, a ridge of shrillness over the clatter and grumble, a gooselike panic of moving sound. She felt impending catastrophe in it all. More than anything she felt the memory in her father's habitual nervousness and preoccupation. Here in the Ritz he was surrounded by people who likely knew who he was, people who had made up their minds about him one way or the other.

It wasn't surprising, thought Evelyn, that the memory seems her own. They had all lived the *Titanic* experience. From the agonizing hours when the ship was swallowed by the ocean, to news—certain reliable news—that Father was saved, through the headlines and articles, artist renditions, some accurate, some wildly at odds with known facts, to the seemingly endless enquiries. They all heard the shrieks of terror and pain, saw the glassy black waters, heard the mighty yawn of the ship as it buckled and sank. They all lived through a different kind of horror at the names Father was called—"loathsome coward," "J. Brute Ismay"—the comparisons between Father and the heroic Captain Smith who went down with the vessel, and the astonishing tidbits—the Montana town called Ismay which debated changing its name to "something less ignominious"—terrifying proof that the idea Father was a traitor had become accepted by all of society.

All this was close enough to her most of the time, was especially vivid tonight. But it was only when she was obliged to shift her seat slightly to get a better view of the band that she knew why the memory had come upon her with such visceral power. Her father, knowing she loved music, encouraged her with a gesture and a brave but false smile as he looked at the musicians and settled back in his chair. Not for the first time this evening she had the distinct impression that what he really wanted was to be left alone with his thoughts. So Evelyn played along, adjusted her position so she could see beyond the splaying leaves of the palm.

A hot, prickling sensation crept up her neck as she listened to the swish of the light jazzy number. It was the bald head of a man on the other side of the plant that claimed her attention first, a coincidental similarity she thought initially—the brown canine eyes, the jowly look with the preoccupied scowl, hardly uncommon in a man of his age. It explained the image that had evoked the *Titanic* and she rested more easily for a moment. But then she leaned to the left, pressing her palm into the table rim for balance, and saw both his wife and daughter, along with a young man unknown to her. The narrow, upward-slanted eyes of the older woman, and her red Celtic hair, were unmistakable. It *was* the Grimsdens. Although she had not seen the Grimsden daughter since she was a spindly child, more than a dozen years ago, she knew the one sitting there, white skin slightly mottled with red, as though from sitting too close to a fireplace, was Miranda, now grown up.

Miranda Grimsden was a name that could conjure demons as effectively as the word *Titanic*. Once, a long time ago, Evelyn had marshalled her own arsenal of words to keep Miranda Grimsden's spell at bay. The newspapers and the enquiries were men's stuff. Father, his solicitors, and his friends would deal with that. Miranda Grimsden's foul little mouth was Evelyn's territory. She gathered all the insults she knew from the schoolroom and the hockey field, garnished them with a few choice phrases picked up second-hand from the gardener's son and from surreptitious reading of some books and magazines on the library's highest shelf. These she had bolstered with words she made up, guttural sounds with vile imagined meanings. In the end, it was not enough; she had never been given the chance to hurl them at Miranda Grimsden.

The lessons of the schoolroom were no doubt right, up to a point. Revenge may feel sour once it is achieved. But being denied vengeance is far worse. It eats you up from inside. In the years after the *Titanic*, Evelyn had been powerless to vent her anger at the obnoxious little girl who had so effectively invaded the inner life of her family. She had been left with no redress.

As she glimpsed the young woman Miranda Grimsden had become, the old anger smouldered afresh. She could remember so precisely the envelope addressed to her father at his home address, with the carefully underlined phrase, "personel and confidentional." Similarly underscored in the missive itself were the little girl's killing words. "*Although I realize I am young and I have no doubt you will think me impertinant to say so, I think that you are* *a <u>coward</u> and a <u>thoughtliss</u> person to have left those poor women and children on the ship while you <u>sneaked</u> off to save your own <u>misrable</u> life."*

It surprises and shocks Evelyn that she can still remember it all word for word, can even conjure the spelling errors and the style of the hand, leaning slightly to the right, cramped and deliberate in the loops, the letters joined self-consciously. She remembers, too, the way the thick, bonded paper had lain upon the table like a felled dove after her father stood, without a word, noiselessly eased back his chair, and walked away from the breakfast table.

ONLY SIX MONTHS BEFORE, the whole Ismay family had made rather a fuss of the girl. The Grimsdens, mutual acquaintances of the Foresters, had been guests at Sunday lunch at their house in Mossley Hill. When the Foresters sent word that one of their party was sick, it had been too late to postpone, and there had been an uncomfortable half hour or so when Mother had been obliged to make awkward small talk with Mrs. Grimsden, under the watchful gazes of the Grimsden daughter and the three Ismay children. The unnatural focus on the back and forth rally of polite trivia had mimicked the atmosphere of a tennis match. The spectators' gazes silently followed the bounce of enquiries and answers. Father had fired a few work-related questions at Mr. Grimsden who answered everything with sardonic monosyllables and a cough, as though he would rather be asked nothing at all. He was Manchester born and bred, and his business was scrap. He rolled the r of the word *scrrrrap* in the way Evelyn had heard Shakespearean actors do.

Mother and Mrs. Grimsden had talked about the weather, always in surprised and delighted agreement, as though it were a revelation known only to the two of them that scattered showers had rather marred a crisp, sunny afternoon the day before yesterday. Mrs. Grimsden talked much more than her husband, but she was similar in the sense that those small, dark eyes seemed to be holding something back.

The symmetry between the two families was obvious, and the likely reason the Foresters advanced the meeting. Father and Mr. Grimsden were both northern businessmen and both had homes in Liverpool, Mr. Grimsden, apparently, because he was exporting *scrrrrap* these days. They were both married to women from somewhere in the Americas, Mother from New York, Mrs. Grimsden from the Nova Scotian capital of Halifax. Evelyn wondered whether this odd similarity caused her reserve, whether Mrs. Grimsden feared the comparison. Her own father had been a shipbuilder too, but she became particularly vague and distant when questions were asked.

"Yes, indeed!" she would reply to Mother in her lilting accent, an American-softened version of Scots. Her expansive smile would withdraw quite unexpectedly and she would gaze off into some middle distance beyond the coffee table. Her poise seemed at once real and exaggerated; Evelyn suspected that her sister Margaret and she would have fun imitating her in private afterwards.

The atmosphere remained brittle, and the silences between words rather intense, until Margaret, bounding off her chair with a sigh, announced she would take Miranda up to the nursery to play with George's train set. Evelyn ran quickly to join them, stopping briefly at the door to ask Mother if she had her permission. Mother nodded gratefully, and as the three girls flitted out of the room, followed by George who was grumbling that no one had asked his permission, the house seemed to relax. Margaret and Evelyn strung bows in Miranda's hair and spun tales for her of daring rescues at sea, encounters with polar bears and sea monsters. The Grimsdens, at least mother and daughter, were planning a summer in New York and would likely travel on one of Father's liners.

Later, during lunch, conversation flowed more easily and there had been the palpable sense of excitement about the upcoming voyage, communicated like a wave from the returning children and taken up by the adults who already seemed more relaxed in each other's company. Mr. Grimsden, who was to stay in Liverpool, relaxed into a different person, slipping fingers into his waistcoat pocket in a rather comical way that Margaret and Evelyn made fun of later and expounding on the necessity of more open trade with the Americas. When he looked at Father now, his dark eyes flickering, Evelyn realized his quietness up to this point had been a form of shyness. He seemed almost boyish as he leaned back in his chair and emphasized a point with a sniff and watched with quiet trepidation to see whether Father would agree. And Father could find a way of sounding like he was agreeing even when an analysis of his words might reveal that he had turned a subtle loop, moving from empathy and affirmation to quiet contradiction.

As it happened, Margaret and Evelyn did not have fun imitating Mrs. Grimsden in the weeks that followed, although they did roll their r's when they mentioned the word *scrap*. The friendly softening toward the Grimsdens had created a quiet sense of loyalty, and the feeling the visit left them all with was wholesome and good.

WHEN MIRANDA GRIMSDEN'S LETTER appeared that September morning, the *Titanic* disaster had been five months in the past. A sense hung over the family that things might never be the same again, but that the duty of one and all was to simulate life as it had once been. An irresistible image emerged from a dream and returned to Evelyn over and over: Mother, Margaret, Evelyn herself and even George scrambling with buckets and spoons trying to scoop water out of a rickety lifeboat. This was their home life as Father moved from being out of reach and silent, to twitchy and distracted most of the time, to finally buckling down to work, and settling into a rhythm the whole family understood.

It had long been his habit to open mail, even bills and business post, at breakfast on weekdays. In one of those quiet and meaningless struggles between husband and wife, Mother had always objected and Father had always persisted regardless. This morning had been no different.

"Bruce, please!" Mother protested as Jenny, the maid, disappeared red-faced after delivering the tray.

"Just a minute," Father had replied, slitting the first envelope, scooping out a bill, then doing the same to a small invitation-sized letter. On seeing the signature first Father had given a brief "ha!" and a playful glance around the table before he read. Only when he rose slowly, letting his napkin fall, did it occur to Evelyn that anything was wrong. He lifted his chair so it wouldn't scrape, turned, and silently left the room.

Mother, Margaret, and Evelyn crowded around the note. George was shooed away. A *tut-tut* from Mother sank slowly into a gloomy, furious silence from all three of them. If Miranda had appeared again before them, Evelyn would gladly have pulled the blue ribbons around the girl's neck and strangled her.

THE FEELING, SO FEROCIOUS at the time, eventually fizzled away into an understanding of its own futility, leaving acrid grime against the inside of Evelyn's memory. There had been nothing to feed it. Lurid and damning editorials from across the Atlantic were swallowed up by more urgent news of the war. In reality Miranda Grimsden's note had been merely a tiny bell ringing the same tune that had clanged mercilessly from other quarters. It had been the unexpected nature of the attack that had made her the focus for Evelyn. She was a little girl. She had been in the house playing with young George's train set. She already dwelt within the soft underbelly of the Ismay home and the stab had been all the more startling. Father had been like a wounded lion, gentle but in his prime respected and revered. Now he was wounded and some beastly little carrion bird—the smallest of the jungle—chirped and mocked at his misfortune.

Only a vague and smouldering sense of loss remained, loss of years traditionally full of joys, gossips, and adventures. Seeing Miranda Grimsden in adult form—her snub nose elongated, her chubby face slimmed into angles and cheekbones—has confirmed her status as a nonentity.

But something sparks afresh, the realization that a nine- or ten-year-old child does not create her biting invective in a vacuum, and that during those intervening years Evelyn would have been better reserving her fury for the proud, small-eyed woman and the barely verbal man who had parented her. The idea is a revelation. A child is a child. Her younger self might have been liberated by the notion had it occurred through the fog of anger and confusion. But now it shackles her more securely than before. Seeing Miranda Grimsden grown up, and ill at ease with her parents, gives context to an almost forgotten tormentor. For the first time she thinks about the accusation as something more than random, more than the misdirected twitch of indignation in an embryonic mind. It was altogether more directed, she realizes, more fuelled; and it absolutely demanded redress.

She wonders for a moment if her father has seen them, whether this is the reason he has been edgy and remote since they sat down to dinner. A quick glance at him, catching a genuine tinge of pleasure in his slightly watering eye as he too listens to the band, makes her realize he could not have. He was never an actor and could not have feigned pleasure while tormentors from his past were so imperfectly shielded from his view.

A moment ago she wanted to reach out and lay her hand upon his as he tapped his fingers upon the table. But that would have given away the fact there was something to worry about. Instead she contented herself with looking until the feeling would make him turn to her, then once this was accomplished, infusing her smile with all the fondness she had for him. He caught her expression, and the sheen of sentiment in his eye was gratitude and warmth, for children and wife, perhaps, and for the home which could not quite be torn asunder by disaster, misfortune and all the accumulated blame of a population in shock and searching for a villain.

chapter three

EVELYN'S ATTENTION IS ALMOST unbearable. One's own child's expectations are so much worse than one's own conscience, he thinks. She wants so much more from him than he wants for himself, and the discomfort of it is rather like that of a long-dead corpse urged back to life against the will of the departed soul. She craves justice, self-respect; she wants him not to give in. And he is so profoundly tired of it all.

Thank God she doesn't appear to have seen them. The chance of a meeting with the Grimsdens, even an accidental locking of eyes, or shuffling sideways of a seat as one of them passes, is horrendous. It would tip the evening into confusion, cause the most brittle of silences to rise between him and his daughter. It would invade their home, no doubt residing there for months in anxious glances in his direction and whispered enquiries about his health.

And with Evelyn one never knows. For him a taboo is a mute object that quivers unacknowledged through its own quiet torments. He isn't sure he can trust Evelyn not to make an open battle of it. And it would be so futile. They would be fighting over a mere reputation, who said what to whom about conduct and honour, and whether it was deserved.

All evening, above the dense murmur of conversation in the Palm Room, a sharper sound has invaded his ears, knife against plate, ice on glass, the occasional shriek of faraway laughter. It was he who chose this place for a quiet dinner, and now he wonders whether it might have been a sort of self-punishment, unconsciously imposed. So many people have been doing battle for years over the wreckage of his soul, why should he not prod the heap himself for a change?

It has never ceased to amaze him that the question of his own conduct brings forth more emotion than the multitude of pointless deaths. It's enough to make a man quite conceited, this idea that his own survival, what he may or may not have said to the captain about the speed of the ship, is worth so much column space when fifteen hundred people died so terribly.

The band has paused between songs, but it is only when Evelyn's rather sentimental expression turns curious, then worried, that he realizes that he is still tapping his fingers on the table even though there is no music.

He's been caught; it's difficult to imagine a more certain proof that his joviality up to this moment has been feigned.

When the band recommences, it's a rather slow, classically styled piece. He recognizes the fragments of melody as an arrangement of Debussy's "Clair de Lune," an odd, rather sombre, choice and not one he would have approved of in the dining room of one of his liners. But musicians can't resist contrast, nor, if the management is too slack, can they stop themselves from attempting to educate an audience.

The talking becomes louder and a little restless in response to the change.

Ismay gives his daughter a shy smile and turns his seat back toward the table. Evelyn holds his gaze for a moment, perhaps deciding whether to chide him for being absent. The path of this conversation has been so well trodden by his wife, Julia, that his daughters and even his sons know it by heart. It starts with a question, often innocently put, something like "Penny for your thoughts?" or "What is your mind so intent upon that you should stare so?" It's a trap, of course, albeit a benign one, and he has never quite reconciled himself to the futility of trying to escape it. He usually pretends he was thinking about something quite unrelated to work—a holiday in the past perhaps, an old acquaintance he hasn't seen for many years. Only the most elaborate of storytellers can get away with such subterfuge, and he, being no such creature, merely becomes evasive, then short-tempered. No one comes out and says it, but silence and a knowing nod confirm the belief that he must have been thinking about some aspect of business present or past. At this point he feels like a criminal.

But tonight is worse. It isn't any normal aspect of work that bothers him. It's *the* night; the one he suspects might be waiting to engulf him once more on the other side of death. He can feel the water lapping gently against the wooden lifeboat shell, he can feel the swell in tune with Debussy, and he can taste the ice crystals on his mouth. What a disadvantage the medieval painters were at when they tried to depict a communal hell. Fire, and brimstone, and cavernous depths will terrify only a portion of the immortal soul; real damnation is more carefully moulded to an individual's experience. His own vision of torment is simple enough: a lifeboat rocking gently upon an ocean; cold; an awareness of people huddled on all sides, a cough here and there, a few words; the idle splash of oar upon the water's surface; a sense that it could not have happened, that the event this group has lived through is too catastrophic, too unbelievable to explain itself to the day, and that time will oblige itself to roll back the hours and restore them all to the *Titanic*, where news of a near miss with an iceberg will bring an enthralling end to a Sunday evening, and the Marconi telegraph operators will fill up the tingling night air with the passengers' tales of romance and adventure.

Before he saw the Grimsdens tonight, he already felt he was on the deck of the great liner slicing through black waters. The gentlest of inclines tilted the soles of his shoes slowly one way, then another, as he and Evelyn stepped from the foyer into the Palm Room. Likely he is on board the *Titanic* every night, he realizes, but seeing the Grimsdens has made him more aware of it than usual.

The wine waiter adds a decorous half inch to Evelyn's glass and refills Ismay's while the soup bowls are removed and the entrées placed before them, hare for father, pheasant for daughter, its singed flesh puckered where the broadest feathers have recently been plucked. Evelyn smiles across the table, letting the expected question drop. Ismay returns the look and raises his eyebrows as though in relish for the feast.

Before drifting from the table, a waiter refills both water glasses. Two wisps of memory now sparkle like floating ice needles, and Ismay realizes both have been present for weeks, tingeing his dreams, and following from a distance during the day. The first recollection is from a memorial service. The hollow sounds of closing hymn books, creaking pews, and suppressed coughs flood over him again. He's at the lectern, reading the lesson, a letter from Saint Paul to the Corinthians about the nature of steadfastness and suffering. As he glances up into the dimmed congregation, he seems to catch something—a faint ironic smile. The impression is too fleeting, too vague for him to be sure it is even real. He looks down again and tries to refocus on the lines, fingers twitching aside the scarlet ribbon; he realizes he can't tell whether the face belonged to man or woman, youth or elder. He stumbles a little before finding the spot, not so markedly that anyone would notice. But it unnerves him, the sense of distrusting his own senses. He has been the subject of enough gossip, the object of enough sniggers to shrug judgment aside while a job is to be done. He is used to enemies, and used to soldiering on regardless. But this is different. He feels that if he looks up again, he might see the smirk once more yet still be unable to pinpoint the direction from which it comes.

The Great War has been over less than a year and this service is for marines lost in the conflict. Ismay has made a very large donation to set up a fund in their memory, much of the money going to their families. For the first time since 1912 he has begun to feel the lifeboat controversy is being overshadowed by something of more practical and immediate importance. He can feel the energy around him change; the murmur that has been following him for seven years is softer, the consonants less hard edged; the eyes that meet his do so with a degree of acceptance, the spark of judgment dying. He is transcending the past, he feels, because the donation is so apt. The people lost are seafaring people, *his* people, quite literally in many cases; personnel from his former ships swelled the ranks of the merchant marines after war broke out. The smirk—or his suspicion of it—disquiets him more than he would have thought possible. It threatens even the concept of atonement.

Yet, he reminds himself at the lectern, the money is real, and the sentiment is real. The donation represents not only himself but family, in-laws, partners, staff, investors, anyone who had ever benefited by mercantile trade and now owes a debt of gratitude. Even if he were to believe the worst said about him, why, he wonders, would his sin subvert an act of such uprightness on behalf of so many?

The second memory is odder and hardly connected at all. It's a party somewhere in New York. He doesn't remember the venue or the host, only the grumble of voices and the angular movements. Clumps of men in evening dress shake hands, gesticulate, tell wild stories to each other and guffaw, before returning to mixed company and behaving quite differently with unexpected poise and formality.

Someone, a lanky fellow, speaks close to Ismay's ear. His voice is sharp, high-pitched, rapid, and Ismay doesn't catch the words. He's aware too late of a white thin-boned hand hovering before him like some exotic flower, and then it disappears. He realizes the man was trying to introduce himself, and half thinks of following and tapping him on the back to make amends for his own slowness, but it is too late; the lanky fellow has joined one of the groups of men, and they receive him enthusiastically with simultaneous yells and two or three outstretched hands.

"Careful, Ismay, there's a guy you don't want to offend." The warning comes from a shipping-agent friend, and is delivered as a joke, or so it seems at the time, although the tone is low, smilingly ominous.

"Who is he?" Ismay asks.

"Hearst, William Randolph. He owns the *San Francisco Examiner* and has just bought *The New York Journal*."

This part of America, despite the propaganda, is stiffer than England, its rules more defined. A man does not meet another man without a handshake and there is no acceptable substitute. The slowness of modesty holds no excuse. Ismay shrugs, knowing it's too late, and supposing the man has already forgotten the unintentional rebuff.

HE STILL SUPPOSES IT now, more than three and a half decades on, as he slices through the brown leg of his hare. After all, that one near-meeting was all that ever happened between them. But like a scattering of stones before a comet hits the earth, the memory in retrospect seems to hold the power of a portent—mystical and strange and utterly disconnected from any real possibility of cause and effect. What a small world, or extraordinary coincidence, or both, that it should have been that very same lanky fellow with the staccato voice and the hovering hand whose newspapers would carry such damning indictments of his own actions, in prose so florid and fantastic he might have enjoyed the sensation of reading if only the subject were not himself. He re-imagines Hearst's narrow, youthful back as he merged into the crowd of partygoers, and wonders if things might have been different if he had obeyed his first instinct and followed, tapped him on the back and tried to engage for half an hour or more on the benefits of Anglo-American trade and commerce.

What an astonishing benefit an open, extroverted personality is, he thinks, with a sullen glance around at diners in nearby tables. To his right, a portly gentleman with slicked back hair laughs at his own joke. The rest of his table, mainly younger men, perhaps business associates, all follow suit. Extroversion, Ismay thinks, is the currency of so much, of friendship, trade, romance, and love. At times it almost seems the measure of virtue. It's a man's calling card and his advertisement; it flows ahead of him in all directions, cementing his reputation, spreading word about his qualities, and perhaps most important of all, securing for him what he may one day need more than anything else: the benefit of the doubt.

"What are you thinking of now, Father?"

So deep is Ismay's unhappy concentration upon the browned mushrooms, mashed potato and dark game, it takes a moment for him to focus properly on Evelyn. When this happens there is no concealing the fact he has been elsewhere. Her knife and fork are lying across her plate and she is like a statue, watching him. This is a trick picked up from her mother: several years ago she started to react to his mealtime silences by calmly giving up on her own food and waiting; when at last he emerged from his thoughts, she would let him guess how long she had been sitting there motionless.

An expression somewhere between concern and exasperation now struggles on Evelyn's face. When she speaks, her voice is quiet, almost conspiratorial. "Don't you think you deserve simply to enjoy yourself without brooding about things, Father?"

The question is invasive. He can feel it carving into his chest cavity, slicing close to his heart. Julia, his wife, knows how to choose a specific detail of his business; most likely these days it would be something to do with a bequest in his will, the inability of his solicitor to get the wording just right to cover all eventualities. But Evelyn has left her meaning gaping with her use of the word *things*, and by her ominous, overly tender tone. Paradoxically, because it specifies nothing, it can have only one meaning: the *Titanic*.

He feels annoyance rising to anger, but falling just as

quickly to nothing. How could he really expect anything different? The *Titanic* is, after all, the knot at the centre of all their lives. She hasn't named the event, poor girl. She doesn't need to.

Evelyn, he suspects, was hoping to keep their conversation this evening to the subject of Basil Sanderson. Ismay knows Evelyn and Basil plan to marry. He knows also that his own approval would mean a great deal to her, but that she is looking for far more than a consent he has already implicitly given. Some kind of dynastic sentiment among his family, touchingly ancient and impractical, longs for healing through marriage lines. With Basil, the White Star Line's likely future chairman, and Evelyn, the house of Ismay would once again be realigned with its proud maritime heritage. Through this plan—and Ismay has no doubt all the appropriate bonds of affection and love came before the other serendipitous aspects of the match—Evelyn and perhaps Julia and Margaret expect a great balm to be applied to the disgrace suffered by himself and the family. In short, they expect it to make him better again.

Ismay tries to greet his daughter's question with an amused smile. "My dear, I am enjoying myself immensely." The sentiment, coming with a genuine-sounding surprise, almost convinces even him. Evelyn sighs gently and smilingly raises her eyebrows. It's the expression of a teacher who has just failed to catch her pupil in the act. They both know of the misdemeanor, the look says, but as it cannot be proven she will drop the matter. Ismay smiles once more, is about to drop his gaze to his plate, when something—an exclamation, a flitting shadow and the clink of glass—makes him turn first to the Palm Room entrance, then to the opposite end of the hall, where there are fresh shrieks and gasps. Evelyn cranes her neck too, catching his eye, questioning. More diners react, looking upward, it seems. Cutlery clinks. The band stops playing. Laughter comes in a wave and a waiter positions himself, silver tray dangling from his hand as though for a catch on the rugby field. All heads turn again in unison, and Ismay, trying to follow the cause of the interest, catches the flick of wings overhead, the darting brown body of a sparrow as it sinks into the foliage of the palm tree closest to them. Some of the men are now on their feet. Three or four waiters converge, hovering uncertainly as they come close to the palm. One claps his hands; the man with the tray waves at the bird with his gloved free hand like a policeman directing traffic.

Ismay realizes he must have shifted his own seat. His view through the palm has changed. Without any obvious cover of leaf or stem he finds himself staring directly into the small, dark eyes of Mrs. Grimsden.

She makes no sign of recognition at first, and neither does he, but the blankness of expression carries a full awareness, even a kind of static acknowledgment, of the situation and the history. Gradually something changes. As the waiters converge gingerly upon the palm and the bandleader counts his musicians off to start again, Ismay neglects to take his eyes from Mrs. Grimsden, not from any desire to face her down, but simply through an inability to think where else he ought to put his own gaze. Her eyes narrow further, and her mouth seems to harden.

If, before this evening, someone had told Ismay that a woman could take "a violent sip of water" he would have told them such an action made no sense, that they were colouring the movements they witnessed with their own fears and prejudices. But this is the only description that aptly conveys the way Mrs. Grimsden now jerks the drink to her lips, tips back her head and returns the glass to the table, her hand still clutching its stem. Still he doesn't look away, this time for a different set of reasons: for one thing he can't; her behaviour is both bewildering and fascinating, so much apparent emotion, such need to express corseted tightly within the constraints of an entirely public setting. Only by forcing malignity into her face and imbuing the most commonplace of movements with a kind of frantic energy can she hope to convey the true level of her indignation. The effect seems vaguely comic, especially with the band now recommencing its program with a jaunty, fast-tempo number. Indeed it *would* be comic, worthy of a scene from a Charlie Chaplin film, if only he were not himself the object of her anger.

He knows what she wants, and does not believe in being pointlessly bullheaded. But to look away now would be giving away something he has yet to concede, although he has been under far greater pressure than this. It would be saying, *Yes, I am a coward and I am ashamed. You have every right to stare and judge.* Even now, after the great trauma of the *Titanic* and the weight of judgment that came down upon him in its wake, he has done himself the service not to buckle in this regard. It is a habit with him now. He will stand his ground until the moment he drops.

His daughter's hand comes upon his arm, compelling him to tear his gaze away at last. She leans across the table with a kind of appeal in her eyes. Of course, he thinks, she has seen the Grimsdens, has likely been aware of their presence all this time, hence the solicitous manner, the open, yet leading, questions—"*What are you thinking about now? Don't you think you deserve to just enjoy yourself without brooding about things?*" He would like to tell her it doesn't matter, that he also has been aware of them all evening, except of course, that it does matter, clearly, and he would never say anything of the kind to his daughter even if it were true. Never have the Ismays talked openly about anything to do with the accusation of cowardice levelled against Ismay after the *Titanic,* nor even about the effect such accusations have had upon him.

Evelyn's eyes are moist, but she is smiling—a fluid, desperate smile.

"Don't worry, Father," she says, turning her eyes pointedly upward toward the chandelier, almost magically drawing his own in the same direction. The sparrow darts one way, then the other, causing the crystal to tingle. "They won't hurt it," she says. They watch together as the bird switches direction again, circling the ceiling fan, then dips, making a young lady duck and shriek with delight. With a flick of the wings it then flies straight as a bullet toward the foyer. The diners break into spontaneous laughter and applause. The waiters still encircling the palm look suddenly redundant and sheepish at the clamor, as though left on stage to receive praise that belongs to another. Evelyn claps, eyes twinkling at her father. Ismay joins in, feeling a genuine kind of relaxation with his laughter, but knowing with that dim instinct for trouble he has always possessed that the relief will not last.

chapter four

MIRANDA MUST HAVE BEEN the only diner in the room not following the course of the sparrow as it flitted around the palm and circled the chandelier. She fixed her stare first at her own fingers on the stem of her glass, then turned to the ornate entrance with the Grecian-looking plants trailing over the gilding, then at a mirror on the far wall, anywhere but at the wretched bird which hovered and ducked between them and J. Bruce Ismay.

Even with her best efforts to try and distract herself, the spellbound faces of the diners and waiters told her where the sparrow was. She could guess at the sight which must have revealed itself to her mother, explaining her ominous change of expression. She took her eyes from the far mirror, glanced at Mother and saw her eyes darken. In spite of herself, Miranda tilted her head far enough to allow her peripheral vision to scan the Ismays' table. There was one person opposite, a young woman in an ivory silk dress. This could only be one of the daughters who had been so nice to her when she and her parents had visited them in Mossley Hill. She now takes a second peek at the dark hair, angular features, and decides it must be Evelyn, the younger of the two, much more grown up than she was at the time, but nearer to being her contemporary all the same.

She could never remember the details, or even much about the event, but the kindness and the fuss, the easy acceptance into the world of older girls had stayed with her. Like a flower in glass, the day was a timeless record of a specific youthful vision; it was her child's conception of the shining adult or near-adult world to which she would one day belong. Everything was felt intensely by Miranda in those days; she categorized events and people as fragments of paradise or of hell. Life as it was, with its long creaking silences in church or in the classroom, was most often dull, belonging decisively to the latter column; the future, however, offered glimpses of something different, a thousand forbidden, sparkling tales, the details of which were always obscure.

She had tried to fill in these details of her imagined worlds, but knew something failed her. Her daydreams always carried the dust and tedium of her own present life. Her heroines were too much like school teachers, exuding the coarse fluff of tweed, speaking too sternly, because she could imagine no other kind of women—

except for her mother, and in those days Mother was a distant, regal figure in her daydreams, too potent to be engaged in the action, but watching from the clouds. The heroes moved and talked with the mannerisms of factory managers, again because she could visualize no other kind of successful man. She tried to paint her sword-brandishing knights with the sheen of glamour, but always a dangling watch chain, a bulging waistcoat, or thinning hair would impose itself upon the picture. She knew herself to be a poor dreamer, and her details always killed the magic. But the Ismay girls had brought her so much closer to the formless vision of paradise that dwelt within her. Their house in Mossley Hill—she already knew they had several, one in Ireland, one in London—was a place of high, curved banisters, muted colours, darkness and wood polish. The train set they brought her up to see was older and clunkier than the ones she had seen before, the tracks wooden and aromatic, and although they were so much older than she was, they approached it all with simple joy, and no sense of ownership or jealousy or any indication they believed it beneath them to play with a train set. They treated her as if she were one of them, and with their soft, pleasant manners, long, slender limbs, hair that shone even in the dimmest light, and scent of unmistakably feminine soap, she longed to be their sister.

She watched Evelyn as she adjusted and retied her bow, gathering strands which glowed like water through her fingers. Miranda sensed somehow the subject of hair was like a secret door giving passage into another world, *their* world, and that if she asked in the right way at the right time, this world would open up to her, at least for the afternoon. When she did pluck up the courage, spilled just a few dry syllables while fingering the wood of a chair leg, it all came so easily she wondered how she could have been nervous about it. Margaret and Evelyn had her sitting in front of the nursery window, brushing her own hair, tying her own yellow and blue bows in a similar style to their own, giggling and arguing in a way that was somehow polite, the way that adults argued, using each other's names—Margaret and Evelyn—nicely, carefully, as though they rather liked the words. There, feeling the gentle pull of the brush, seeing her strands of hair fall against the sunlight, intense through the window, she felt she was entering into a magical universe.

The only thing worse to her than coming face to face with Mr. Ismay again would be coming across him in the company of one or more of those pretty daughters who had once been so nice to her. She wonders now whether it was precisely *because* they had been so pleasant to her that she acted as she did. Such things are written about so often these days; one has only to pick up a newspaper to hear some secondhand account from an Austrian psychotherapist who believes people are compelled to act in a way directly contrary to their own best interests and desires. Were the minds of women and men always so tangled? she wonders. Or is this a recent thing brought about by too many jolts, like a poison floating in the ether after an explosion? As she tries to make sense of the idea, she remembers another afternoon, weeks after the *Titanic*, a restful hotel suite in New York, overlooking the great rolling park. She hears again the rustle of newspaper pages on carpet, an unendurable sound to her normally, but today, on her knees, scissors in hand, she is forcing herself to endure it. She has been cutting out words from a slightly yellowed copy of *The Denver Post*, dated 19 April 1912. Mr. Johnston brought it with him when he arrived the day before yesterday with parcels of new clothes for her and her mother, and he read it aloud. The article, he told her, was written by his boss, and although it mentions no names at all, Mother later assured Miranda, through hushed lips, that it was about Margaret and Evelyn's father. It talks of the nobility and self-sacrifice of the brave men who looked after women and children and then stood calmly upon the deck of the *Titanic* as they went down to glory. "Who," the article ends by asking, "would not rather die than live a coward?" Miranda understands, but only just, that this must be the part about Mr. Ismay.

    The article itself has now been reduced to meaningless phrases like "500 feet in the air," "that the," "might be," "lapse of years," "would not rather," while the words which carry emotion and promise drama—"graves," "disaster," "desolate," "children," "glorious," "kissed," "doomed," "hero," "coward," and she thought for good measure, as the lettering was so large and in bold, the author's name, Mr. Johnston's boss, "WILLIAM," "RANDOLPH," and "HEARST"—are all either scattered on the carpet or glued onto a flat, square piece of cardboard she cut from a gift package.

Miranda's experiment is to cut out and randomly select words from the article, creating, she hopes, a new and revelatory meaning upon the cardboard surface. All of this is done by touch; her eyes are closed. Already she has it in her head that she might emerge from the experiment with a coded message, one of comfort perhaps, which might be sent to the Ismay girls. Even her mother, who is definitely in agreement with the article's author, has expressed regret at the suffering some of the press coverage might have caused the girls and their mother.

When Miranda opens her eyes, she sees a hodgepodge of words, some, from the headline and from the writer's name, large and blocky; some, from subheadings, like little brothers to the blocky ones; and some, from text too insignificant, by comparison to the bolder script, to notice. This seems unfair, as it was these—"coward," "monuments," "self-sacrificing"—that made her pulse race with the promise of some kind of answer, some revelation for which she is searching. It's a disappointment, and now, hearing murmurs of her mother and Mr. Johnston from the living room of the suite, her heart picks up with a little fear.

Mother has not specifically told her she should *not* cut up the gift box from Mr. Johnston's extra little present to her mother—the rose set in glass—but she can be oddly sentimental about such things, especially with Mr. Johnston. A strange and rarified air seems to hang around her when the two of them are together, and Miranda is frightened of the change. Mother's eyes seem both intently focused on Mr. Johnston yet far away from everything, as though she's a woman in a painting dreaming of some distant mountain range. She has taken to speaking differently too, enunciating more carefully and rising to a sing-song pitch. There is more fuss about her clothes and jewelry, or Miranda is noticing it more; she applies lipstick more carefully and more often, and Miranda hears the clicking of pearls and the ruffling sound of the whitish dress she's recently purchased for herself with its many fairy-like folds. This all suggests that everything, even cardboard boxes and newspapers, may have become precious and important, dipped as they must have been in this enthralling dream that seems to have descended upon her world. Miranda imagines the horrified expressions on both of their faces if Mother and Mr. Johnston were to come into the nursery now and see the mess she has made with Mr. Johnston's newspaper and with the gift box.

Frantically she begins to gather it all together, unused

paper hissing against the carpet as she tries to scoop all the scraps into the remains of the box, along with her own pasted sections upon the cardboard square. The word "coward" stares at her, white glue seeping from under its bottom right corner. Although the letters loom at her as an accusation, the word carries her thoughts like an arrow far away, across the ocean, skimming past Mr. Ismay—the writer's intended target—merely ruffling his hair a little as it flies, then sinking quite unexpectedly into the fond old chest of her father as she sees him in her imagination, slumped forward at his study desk, dozing. It unsettles her, and she immediately tries to remember him in attitudes of authority, seeing how his employees approach him, with soft treads and deference, nodding at his words and colouring slightly as they speak. He's a powerful man, a brave man, she tells herself, yet visions of her mother like a great, mocking butterfly—a cabbage white in that rustling dress of hers—interfere. She hears the laughter of Mother and Mr. Johnston from the suite's living room.

AS THE GENERAL LAUGHTER at the poor bird's departure dies into titters, Miranda begins to rummage in her head for topics that will keep her mother from the inevitable. She knows it's useless even to try, that when it comes to words her own arsenal would be like a pistol opposing an army of tanks.

She latches on to the sight of the waiters returning to

their posts, the tray dangling from the gloved hand. The silver catches the chandelier lights in a way that's quite painful. "I don't know what the waiters were hoping to do," she says hastily and mainly to Graham. "They looked more afraid than the poor bird."

As soon as the words leave her lips, she realizes the danger. She has left an opening for her mother.

"Some men are afraid of everything," Mother says in a voice designed to carry far beyond the table.

Before she came to England and married, Mother said she had acted upon the stage in Halifax, and in times of emotional stress she still has the uncanny ability to throw her voice without yelling. It's quite impossible to ignore her, and Miranda knows that the quizzical silence from Father and Graham will stretch time and focus attention from all around upon the speaker. Mother bends the laws of physics. It doesn't matter that, in a technical sense, the silence runs forwards, rather than backwards, in time. The words will hang in the air, leaving their imprint. In the hush around it, Miranda can't imagine how the Ismays will fail to hear.

chapter five

EVELYN FEELS IT SWEEP through her in short, strong pulses: the imperative of it, the knowledge that she must now act. Her head becomes muffled—in a separate world entirely from the glass by her hand, the food on her plate, the lights overhead, and the ornate mirrors—yet keenly alert. Every sound, every laugh and murmur of conversation, every clink of silver and china merges into a single urgent battle-drum rhythm.

It's no longer *whether* she'll challenge the Grimsdens—she knows she must—but rather *how* she'll choose her moment. And this is delicate. There is no doubt that Father has heard the comment; she can see it in the flicker of his eyes, the sudden stoop in his shoulders as he goes back to cutting his meat; it's not the hunched look of apology or guilt, but rather a stoical, bullish posture of one who is used to bearing great weight without complaining. Despite this, because he has already suffered so much, her duty now is to answer the Grimsden woman without involving him. And it has to be possible. She has to move from her table eventually, and Evelyn can make her own excuses to follow into the foyer before her father can catch up.

This much she can plan. But then what? Various scenes play out in rapid succession. She sees herself tugging at the woman's stole with one hand and slapping her across the face with the other—a richly rewarding moment no doubt, but one that would look utterly insane to those who would inevitably bear witness to the act. She remembers also from childhood that a blow that seems clean-cut and decisive upon conception, can become an ugly tangle of limbs when the idea moves into reality. Isabelle Dryden once said Evelyn's friend Jessica, then nine years old, was a "trollop." After checking in the library dictionary for the meaning of the word, Evelyn, who liked to be methodical and organized, mapped out her moves as though arranging a duel: first she would call out the girl's name and tell her why she was being punished, then she would pause, allowing Isabelle to defend herself, then she would strike with her right hand across Isabelle's left cheek. She went through it so many times; she managed to convince herself this was how it would unfold. But Isabelle did defend herself, and somewhat better than Evelyn had anticipated, beating her to the first blow. The two descended into a heap of kicks and pinches and got themselves into trouble when they reappeared in class with mud on their clothes. She imagines now the equivalent between herself and Mrs. Grimsden, the broken buttons, the disarranged hair, the scattered pearls, and knows this kind of revenge belongs decisively to the worlds either of childhood or low comedy.

But Mrs. Grimsden, unlike Isabelle, would be a sitting target. And the opportunity might come. Her own father might excuse himself, freeing Evelyn to cross the restaurant floor to the Grimsdens. Words, she knows, would be quite beyond her. This is the problem with anger and injustice. It robs one entirely of the ability to construct thoughts into logical argument. It turns one into a savage. Even the modest accusation she managed against Isabelle Dryden seems beyond her now. The only act she can imagine at the end of the ten- or twelve-pace walk to the Grimsden table is the sudden picking up of a glass and the throwing of the contents over Mrs. Grimsden's head. Even then her fury might make her aim unreliable.

She can envision the reaction, and in great detail: she can see the surprised look on Agnes Grimsden's face as Evelyn appears before her. She can hear the gasp of outrage and shock as the liquid sinks into her hair and dribbles down her cheeks onto the table. She can imagine Mrs. Grimsden calling to her husband, the stunned silence that would overtake the room, the mute panic of the waiters, Mr. Grimsden standing in horror, perhaps throwing his serviette onto the table but being utterly lost as to how to respond as the assailant is, after all, a woman.

She would brave it all, she feels, even if it meant arrest and trial, and is quite certain of her mettle in this respect. It seems an incongruity, rather than a contradiction, that she has been unable even to look in the direction of the Grimsdens since hearing the comment. If she were to catch sight of those small eyes, she thinks, the thin, still rather handsome face of Agnes Grimsden, one of two things would happen. She would either look away suddenly—that most involuntary and fatal of gestures would be unforgivable on its own account, and would sap the courage and determination that had been building—or the meeting of eyes would precipitate swift and urgent action, whether it was the right moment or not.

The battle-drum rhythm turns into an ache of fear. She's afraid of disgracing herself in public by going too far, but more afraid of dishonouring her father by not going far enough.

Quite suddenly, a movement beyond the palm catches her eye. She does look up now, and urgently, as the two men at the Grimsden table and one of the women are standing. What if they are leaving? A jolt goes through her, not so violently that Father would notice, but it's enough to bring the battle rhythm back to her chest. Now she sees the woman, Miranda, is merely excusing herself. Mr. Grimsden and the young man resume their seats.

She watches Miranda Grimsden moving uneasily down the aisle between the tables, head hanging, one shoulder higher than the other as she grips her purse, like someone with spinal problems, or perhaps someone trying to be invisible—a shy butterfly just emerged from its cocoon, too aware that the silken green of her dress is drawing many eyes. It's an imperfect opportunity. Miranda is a secondary target at best, Evelyn thinks, as she lays her knife and fork gently across her plate. But for the time being it's all she has.

"Excuse me, Father," she says with a smile as she rises. Her father returns her smile, seems reassured by her softness at first, but she catches a look of anxiety just before she turns.

As she follows, Evelyn sees patches of Miranda through the bustle of waiters and sidecars. She notices her head is less drooping, her shoulders less uneven, and now knows for sure it was her father and herself that made her feel cowed. The attendant opens the outer door to the bathroom and Miranda goes through with a distracted-looking nod. The door closes again and Evelyn hesitates, wondering what exactly she will say when she comes face to face with Miranda Grimsden. She's close enough now for the attendant, a ginger-haired girl dressed in black with a white apron, to register confusion about whether she means to enter. It's to satisfy the girl, rather than any other consideration, that Evelyn presses on. Once through the squeaking outer door, she finds the space is darker and silent. An older lady attendant stands within the little vestibule, waiting to open the inner door to the bathroom. A shiver rises up Evelyn's neck as this second attendant reaches for the handle. The door makes no noise opening and Evelyn comes into a blue-marbled space. Electric lights create a steady wash of bright reflections. White, gold-tapped sinks arch like swans' necks in a line, and a tuneful *blop, blop* of water echoes throughout the space.

At the far wall two attendants stand very still with towels draped over their forearms. Miranda is at the farthest sink, her purse nestling next to the tap. She stares into the mirror, unscrewing her lipstick, but Evelyn can tell her attention is elsewhere; her hands seem fidgety and nervous, her bare arms rigid and blotchy even under the blue light. The fact that she does not look around, makes no motion at all about her shoulders to do so, confirms that Miranda Grimsden knows who has followed her.

This is virgin water for Evelyn. She has no sense of the protocols and procedures required, but finds herself marching straight ahead past the first, second, third sink, to the one directly adjacent to Miranda. She catches a confused blink from one of the forward-staring attendants, and knows the atmosphere she has brought with her is far from casual. It must be very obvious the two customers are not from the same party, but that between them lies a history. Evelyn lays her own purse next to the tap and unclips its clasp. Staring at herself in the mirror, she's surprised at how little agitation she sees; the eyes in the glass meet hers steadily, her hair is not disarranged and the movement of her fingers as she takes out her mascara betrays no visible tremors. She feels, rather than sees, a tip of Miranda's head in her direction like that of a tortoise peeking over the ridge of its shell to assess some danger. Only when she applies the first licks to her lashes does Evelyn realize she has been holding her breath. Now the air oozes out of her like the wind from a creaking bellows, and she puts the mascara brush down, suspecting nerves might spill over at last.

Evelyn catches the furtive beginnings of a turn from Miranda Grimsden, suspects she may be on the verge of slinking away, and knows that, to prevent her mission from descending into futility and cowardice, she must do or say something, and quickly.

"Miranda Grimsden," she says. Punctuated by the resonant *blop, blop* of water from the stalls behind them, Evelyn's words seem to have emerged without much effort from some dreamy netherworld. The tone is commonplace, rich in the echoing chamber of the room, a touch disparaging perhaps but not particularly accusing. Still, she can feel the unnatural stillness beside her as she replaces the mascara and roots aimlessly through the contents of her purse with her fingertips. She has, at least, prevented Miranda's escape.

"Yes."

The answer is an odd surprise, almost startling in fact. "So," she says, having no idea at all how to continue. Pantomime phrases push themselves into the front of her mind: *We meet again; you thought you could escape me; we have ways of dealing with the likes of you.* She's suddenly aware of the absurdity of following Miranda Grimsden to the bathroom. They are no longer children, yet the only logical reason for a confrontation would be to pressure the girl to disown the letter she wrote to her father thirteen years ago. What a shameful admission, that the ramblings of a ten-year-old invaded her family to such an extent! Her face, still locked upon her own reflection, burns at the thought. Thankfully the redness does not show through the wash of blue light.

"I heard your mother," she merely says, taking herself by surprise again.

She hears an intake of air, and turns her head far enough to see Miranda's arm frozen on her purse, her head down, her eyelids flickering.

"I thought you would," she says.

It takes a moment to register that this is not an apology—everything about it, the tone, and posture says that it is—and another moment to realize that she prefers this to the conventional "sorry." There's anticipation as well as regret in *I thought you would*. It disarms Evelyn for a moment, and deflates her too. It *is* absurd to have followed Miranda Grimsden in here, the act of a nursery battle that takes upon itself an argument between parents, while the parents themselves remain oblivious and aloof. But there is a purpose. In the barren ground of this meaningless, aborted conflict her arguments are forming with perfect clarity and order. She is counting the fallacies that became accepted truth: her father *did* help with the lifeboats until his help was no longer needed or required; he took *nobody's* space as the lifeboat was already being lowered; he asserted *no* pressure upon the captain to increase his speed—this was the most oft repeated and groundless of the accusations; her father had over and over again warned against early arrivals as an inconvenience to passengers and merchants alike, who must then scramble for either an extra night's accommodations or a warehouse for goods at the last moment.

And Evelyn can tie these falsehoods together with the ribbon of an overarching truth, the reason for her father's misrepresentation. Once a man slips into the role of a scapegoat, grief, infamy, and distortion will conspire to weave every strand of evil intent from his supposed actions. There is simply too much stray, unhappy energy for it to be otherwise. It all has to find a home somewhere and J. Bruce Ismay was the home.

All of these arguments could now easily be unburdened as she and Miranda Grimsden stand before the mirrors, clicking and unclicking their purses and compacts, raising and lowering lipsticks and mascara brushes with the music of dripping water around them. The sparse but telling communication between them thus far has convinced Evelyn that the Grimsden girl would merely listen and acquiesce. But what would be the point? The enemy is elsewhere, carelessly and confidently sitting in the dining room, saying what she pleases to whomever's ears can be reached.

Sensing the Grimsden girl shift—a slow, bovine movement from her shoulders as she picks up her purse—Evelyn burns with fresh shame and annoyance. Her imagined eloquence, she knows, has merely been lured forward by the timidity of her supposed opponent. If she confronted the woman, Miranda's mother, who has had the boldness to gather all the vindictiveness levelled at Father into that single sentence, she would be reduced to grunts and blows.

Evelyn turns, following the circle Miranda makes around her, a noiseless inner growl her only comfort. The attendant skips ahead to open the door. But just as it seems Miranda will make a faceless retreat and disappear, she stops, turns fully toward Evelyn for the first time, forearm protectively across her belly, hand fidgety upon the opposite elbow.

"I'm sorry about it, really," she says, apparently sincere in a glib and sulky way. "But there's nothing to be done with Mother." Then she colours as though realizing something, looks away and then back again. "Sorry about the letter too. I wasn't really in my right mind, I suppose. You can tell your father that." She does turn finally now, stooping as she makes her way through the door which the attendant has kept open for her. The attendant, a dark-haired woman of about thirty, closes the door and remains where she is, towel still over her forearm. Her eyes flicker, avoiding Evelyn's gaze.

chapter six

THE LIGHTNESS AROUND HER shoulders, as Miranda makes her way back to her seat, feels like euphoria, the heady, exhausted kind experienced at a funeral when the departed has been ill and bed-ridden for many years. But there's an undeniable jingle to it, a flighty, feather-swift quickening of the pulse in time to the ragtime rhythm of the band, a timorous excitement at the flutter of a lady's fan as she passes. Free at last, she thinks, and inwardly she congratulates herself.

All evening, since spying Mr. Ismay, she has been too afraid to leave her seat, but her mother's declaration made hiding impossible. There was suddenly only one course she could take. She must draw out the accuser and get it all over with. And what surprised her most was the sudden thrill of the idea, nestling within the terror like an exquisite blossom within a pile of broken glass. If she could get through a confrontation, if she could outface her younger self, disown it with some kind of apology, some sign of recompense, it would be like eradicating a poison that has sapped her strength for so long she can barely remember life as it was before.

She knew she would be followed. She understood the subtle transfer of energies that existed in public spaces—who noticed whom, who was drawn to whom—and assumed it must be something in her blood, a trait she had inherited from Mother. Actors and actresses understood people, had a sense of the magnetic-like forces that commanded attention and spurred excitement. There was something inherently dishonest, even cowardly, about the retreat designed to draw forth a pursuer and give oneself the opportunity to relent. And the moment the Ismay girl came through the bathroom door, shimmering ivory dress bluish in the bathroom light, she felt both ashamed of the device and excited by the power of her own instinct. It was a courtship of a kind, an ancient pattern known in classical and medieval rhymes, the hunter disguising herself as the hunted, and she partly despised herself for it even while she basked in the relief of her success.

Miranda catches sight of her mother, whose eyes shine with that strange guarded pleasure as she speaks to her prospective son-in-law, and suddenly wonders what else she might have inherited from her. Miranda knows herself to be quite unlike her mother in the more obvious ways, reticent in company while her mother seems formidable, boyish and sober in dress while her mother veers toward the flamboyant and feminine. Tonight, only, Miranda has made an exception with silken green, a compliment of sorts to her mother's mint green sewn with onyx gemstones. Though her dress is plainer than her mother's garb, she rather regrets even this much compromise as it draws more eyes than she is used to.

The differences between mother and daughter are notable enough, Miranda thinks. But a shudder of fear moves through her as she sits, catching her mother's inevitable half-questioning, potentially disapproving glance, and shrinks under its influence. She is, and always has been, terrified of the woman known to the outside world as Agnes Grimsden, has always personified her as an awaiting catastrophe. The sparkle of gold, diamond, and pearl seems uncannily akin to the carefully arranged glasses and dinnerware on board the *Titanic* itself; she imagines the dreadful buckling, twisting, smashing sounds building to a cacophony were her mother to tip from her chair and slip to the ground.

But her mother is only part of Miranda's terror. It's also the manifold similarities between them that might be hidden beneath the surface. Shyness is not a character trait; it's merely an absence of words in a given situation. If one were to remove her inhibitions, who is to say what other differences might evaporate? Dressing boyishly, for instance, is as much the fashion today as adornments were in Mother's era. She shares her mother's frightening ability to read people, to know what will lure them, and what scares and depresses them. And when Miranda did act that one time against the Ismays, it was her idea, not her mother's, even though the sentiments may have been borrowed from her parent.

Even while Miranda tries to seek refuge in Graham's mildly concerned smile, her mother tries to hold her gaze, and she realizes another reason why her fear might be peaking. She's committed an act of betrayal.

Her eyes duck to her plate, back to Graham, avoiding Mother's for the moment while she runs through her own words to Evelyn Ismay and their implications. *There's nothing to be done with Mother*. She imagines her mother hearing the words as she spoke them, imagines her scooping straight into her own recent memory of the event, reading her thoughts. How profoundly unsayable the simple sentence seems now, like an obscene gesture made against a cathedral altar during the quietest hush of a service.

Loyalty to family, and particularly to Mother, has always been extreme. And Miranda feels it not as some shackle foisted upon her, but rather as a *part* of her, a muscle at the core of her heart responding to the urgent need for life-giving blood. She remembers the freezing deck once more, feels her mother's protective power in the bristling fur of her coat, a great mother bear protecting her young, towering proudly as she eases Miranda forward from the high lip of the great ship onto the lifeboat suspended a terrifying distance from the water.

"Don't look down, Miranda. Look straight ahead." Her hands were warm and protective on Miranda's shoulders as she moved onto the lifeboat. "Make room for my daughter, please," Mother's voice warns, and a space opens before her, hands reaching up to steady her onto a low seat. Mother stands for a moment, dignified, unafraid, and then settles beside her. Miranda gazes back onto the deck as men scuttle around, their shoes shining under the deck lights, trousers comically flaring as they bend and crouch and turn the clanking iron wheel of the lifeboat support. The boat deck is no longer level, and even Miranda knows this can't be right. For something as huge as the *Titanic* to tilt even a little is like the moon disappearing from the heavens on a cloudless night. It can mean nothing good. She sees the concentration in the face of one of the sailors, a blue vein running along his forehead as he turns the crank, eyes moist with the cold, staring straight ahead. She wonders about him, whether he is thinking of himself, his family back home. Perhaps he has a daughter too. When her thoughts stray onto her father, she's hit by a wave of emotion so painful she can hardly bear it. She sees him at the Ismay dinner table, deferring in that odd, quiet way of his—a combination of tight-lipped northern pride and cow-eyed need for approval—

remembers the twinkle appearing in his eye as Mr. Ismay talked of the luxury of the liner upon which Miranda and her mother were booked.

"They'll be travelling first class, of course," Father told Mr. Ismay, his voice slightly defensive, fingers creeping into his waistcoat pocket.

"Of course," said Mr. Ismay, his voice soft, reassuring, as though humouring a child.

Father sniffed, nodding.

Her father's vulnerability was poignant, saddening even to the nine-year-old Miranda. How dreadful, how unendurable it would be, she thought, to see him upon the deck with the other fathers and husbands—some waving handkerchiefs jokingly, others pensive, one or two smiling sadly then suddenly looking away—as the lifeboat jolts downwards, the deck slipping away.

"Women and children only," yells an officer now out of sight, and Miranda hears footsteps scuttling along the deck to the next available lifeboat.

MIRANDA LOOKS AT HER father now, remembering, watches him take a sip of water then go back to his meat, his thoughts no doubt far from the table, at the office, thinking of exports at one of the factories, thinking of new equipment or productivity. Gratitude for his safety comes over her shoulders like a warm blanket, but she feels a prickle and shiver of breeze too.

On the other side of the palm, Evelyn returns to her table. Miranda catches sight of her swooping ivory dress from beyond the palm. She glimpses the smile too, warm, generous, purposeful. Mr. Ismay looks up and smiles too, a touch nervously perhaps, the ghost of a question in his eyes.

If I still feel protective toward my own father after all this time, Miranda thinks, *how must Evelyn Ismay feel? Would she really be satisfied?* An answer comes back straightaway: of course not. One perfunctory and very late unburdening of guilt; how could it satisfy anybody?

Mother laughs at something Graham has said, something Miranda didn't catch. Miranda locks eyes with her for a moment. The feeling she is a traitor returns and, along with the guilt, a kind of twisted satisfaction. Mother's laugh was the forced yet luxuriating kind that can't help but draw attention from other tables. Miranda realizes how effectively her own words to Evelyn have reinforced Mother as the target. And something about Evelyn's movements as she returned to her father's table, something about her smile too, suggests unfinished business.

chapter seven

THERE'S SOMETHING IN EVELYN'S smile, a quality profoundly warm and caring and focused on his welfare, which makes Ismay feel very old. He can't place exactly when the balance tipped, making his children protectors and himself the one to be looked after, but suspects it was a slow reaction to events thirteen years ago, that the change was set in motion then, and the vision he has just seen—healthy young woman, soft lines of anxiety hidden beneath an indulgent smile—carries the tingling certainty of a premonition.

He sees himself in the not-so-distant future: an old man with a tartan blanket over his legs. He gazes absently at a bed of tulips as someone in a nurse's uniform wheels him along the gravel path. The windows of a high-walled institution stare coldly down upon them, ivy trailing along the bricks and toward the ledges. Evelyn herself might be a nurse walking toward them with a tray, bottle, and spoon.

"There, there, Mr. Ismay. Your medicine."

He would like to fight against all this but knows there will soon come a point in life where the battle will be beyond him. The shields, swords, and banners of real life are already passing from his grasp. And, since 1912, it always was too private a battle to share. He has been the aging warrior who will not compromise his position of sole leader in the attack. The change, when it becomes apparent to the outside world, will be a sudden one. One moment he will outstare his foe, the next he will be in the mud, his arthritic hand twitching some way from his bayonet.

He examines Evelyn's face as she smiles once more and settles into her seat. A more immediate worry does, at least, subside. Evelyn was always a person of poise, a sensible person, but for thirteen years he has lived in dread that a child of his may one day be drawn into some unnamable conflict of shrieks and blows on his behalf. When he noticed that Evelyn was leaving the table on the heels of Miranda Grimsden, a twinge of suspicion went through him. The timing might be more than coincidence. Then, as he sat alone, watching Evelyn's shimmering form move around the tables toward the ladies' cloakroom, the rolling power of a nightmare descended.

In recent years he has struggled with the same night terror, not exactly a dream as he is never fully asleep when it occurs; but an imagined scene that leaves the aftertaste of nightmare, the same acrid breath: Tom, Margaret, Evelyn and young George as they were when children—George in a sailor suit, gollywog in his hand, the girls in the white pinafores and ribbons they used to wear to church—huddle together in a rocking lifeboat. Nothing else is visible but the moving ripples of moonlight illuminating the boat's planking and the folds of the girls' dresses. But there is a distant sound, first a few, faint falling cries, like seagulls far away. Then the sound grows as though from a large gathering flock. The children huddle closer to each other, and Margaret stares over the rim of the boat. The cries continue to multiply and draw nearer; and then he can hear distinctly human syllables: *or, ard, tray, or cow, tray.* Each time he strains to make them out. And then he catches them. "Traitor! Coward!" And they repeat and grow louder, circling the lifeboat. He waits for hands to grip the deck rail, but however loud the cries, this never happens, and the boat never moves beyond the gentlest of sways.

Each time he hears the voices, it is like the first time, even though the scene has been played out many times before. And though he knows it is he who has earned the accusations, he knows also that the voices do not care; his children are his heirs and, as such, are held responsible for his crimes.

Ismay returns his daughter's smile, trying to remember whether this waking dream visited him last night. He decides it must have done; it seems so vivid he can almost feel the tip of the lifeboat bottom beneath his chair, can almost see the band of moonlight rippling over Evelyn's dress.

"Will you miss London when you go back, Father?"

Evelyn takes a sip of wine and waits for the answer. Ismay recognizes a friendly duplicity in the question, a need to get him thinking beyond this time and place—the restaurant, the Grimsdens, being recognized, business matters that still require him to come into the London office from time to time.

"You know me, my dear," he replies, attempting a reassuring smile. "I'm happy where I am these days, pottering about and whatnot. As long as your mother is with me and my children can visit."

"And will there be good hunting this autumn?" she asks with a fake Irish accent and a touch of mischief in her eye. It's a relief, this return to her usual teasing form. Both Evelyn and Margaret rib him, making out that since retiring he is trying on the new persona of an Irish country squire.

"Let's see what the local gamekeeper can rustle up!"

It's not entirely without foundation. Ismay does hunt occasionally in Connemara and likes it more than he would have believed possible. There's something reassuring about carrying a gun, its weight in his hands, solid, reliable. He likes the fact that hunting requires him to walk long distances, take the fresh air, and really notice the breeze and the trees and the curves of the landscape. Most of all he likes the ritual—the cleaning of the barrel, the rod, the polishing of the butt, the endless talks with staff, and the visitors who care little about his past.

The question almost rescues him, nearly puts him in tune again with the swinging rhythm of the band. But just as his spirits rise and his vision begins to scan the restaurant, he catches her eye again: Mrs. Grimsden lifting the drink to her lips. She seems farther from him now, though he knows it is physically impossible, an illusion brought about by the shielding plant. Her stare carries not so much indignation as before but rather reveals the colder side of anger.

He's reminded of something he'd almost forgotten, so buried as it was in the many accusations labelled against him—the "cheap brittle steel" of the *Titanic* hull plating, his mad pursuit of profit at the expense of safety, the criminal reduction in lifeboat allocation, the panic he was supposed to have displayed as the boats were lowered. Though Mrs. Grimsden herself never testified at the inquest, she was very friendly indeed with a lady who did. She also had, he recalled, been part of the same conversations on board from which the witness drew her assumptions. He had read the transcript of her testimony so many times he had it memorized.

No, the witness kept repeating. She did not actually

hear Mr. Ismay say they were trying for a speed record, but it was the general impression he seemed to give, that they intended to speed through the ice.

He'd said no such thing, of course, but the transcript irked him. It was a thorn of injustice, a flagrant untruth on top of so much else he had to consider. The transcript made it clear that the phrase "general impression" drew the questions like spilt honey will draw a cluster of wasps. The chairman circled the evidence over and over as though it were vital, though he was likely just trying to get to a single fact. It was reported on with such thoroughness, such persistence, that the public must have been given little choice but to believe this was the nub of the matter, Ismay's insistence on speed. "A general impression" ended up having more credence than a proven fact.

Who were all these strange creatures who spun details from inference and invention? The trouble is, and always was, that Ismay could never really understand it—the motivation from the individual's point of view. He could understand why collectively they all needed someone to blame. There was symmetry to the idea. Like gathering frost crystals that form recognizable patterns on a window pane, a system of enquiry was bound to yield something specific, to hone into a single point of blame. Why not him? He was, after all, ultimately in charge of the whole operation, and an unimaginable disaster had occurred under his leadership.

There was even a strange kind of comfort in it. The accusations kept pace with the frantic pulse of his thoughts. He questioned his faith in the Siemens-Martin formula for steel plating. Was it cost and only cost that had made him a convert? At the Belfast dockside, foremen and engineers alike referred to the plating as "battleship strength." Was this merely because Ismay was present? Did they suppose this was the answer he wanted to hear?

In the months after the disaster Ismay would rattle feverishly through drawers at four in the morning, finding, reading, and re-reading the letters, searching for hidden meaning, for opportunities to confirm he was the culprit. He read through Thomas Andrews' memos and letters about the number of lifeboats. Before the disaster Andrews' query had sounded half-hearted to him, like a man who merely wished to be reassured it was all right to reduce the number of lifeboats when he, too, preferred the idea of unencumbered deck space. Ismay felt at the time he was merely helping to snip away some red tape. Now, with the *Titanic* gone, it all seemed more open-ended. Andrews was asking for leadership, and what did he give?

All the decisions seemed right at the time, as Julia kept telling him, trying to control her impatience and desperation. But in point of fact, of course, they were wrong. This was the problem. Who, ultimately, could disagree with that simple analysis? And who could carry the blame if not the person who had made those decisions?

If anyone could have found a way to squeeze wisdom from it all it would have been his father. Yet there was a conundrum; the notion of a disaster of *Titanic*'s scale while his father lived and presided as chair was simply unthinkable. Catastrophe—real catastrophe involving heart-rending tears and desperation—could not exist in the same space as someone as indomitable as Thomas Ismay. Ismay caught this belief in the censorious shake of the head of some of the older directors in the meetings Ismay chaired after the *Titanic*. If the *Oceanic* had struck an iceberg, his imagination had them thinking, Thomas would have kept the ship afloat by sheer strength of character. No doubt their judgment of him was all wrapped up with the accusations of cowardice, but loss was their concern, financial loss and the stability of the company. His willing death would have made no difference to that.

Ultimately it hardly mattered why he was blamed. As a child he had been struck by an image of St. Sebastian in a Religious Studies school book. Tied to a stake, face contorted with pain, a dozen fiery arrows stuck out of him. It served a purpose for the world, this ritual slaughter, he knew now. Ismay daily faced the arrows from outside and from within. Without them, without the scorching heat of distraction, he would have gone insane.

Still, while he is inured to the arrows, Mrs. Grimsden and her type mystify him. The individual's role in creating blame is distasteful somehow, like a leer before the scaffold, the pull of the condemned's feet to hasten strangulation.

For the second time tonight he doesn't take his eyes from her, and for the second time tonight her stare seems to grow in indignation. And then something happens which is both new and unexpected, an emotion rising on the heels of his memory of Mrs. Grimsden's friend and her "general impression." The feeling gathers strength and sensation—the taste of April 15, the ice whiskers in the air, the hubbub, the growing panic and confusion upon the deck, and the odd, elongated silence after a flare hissed into the crystal black sky.

Ismay laughs.

It's merely the physical response to absurdity, unfiltered by logic or intellect. The silly, pointless lie from Mrs. Grimsden's friend, the stare he's confronting now from the lady herself seem akin to scavengers picking over a battlefield. One bends to remove the gun from a severed hand as cannon smoke drifts and curls. Another tugs upon an ammunition belt, trying to loosen the strap. What's a hostile stare to fifteen hundred lives lost? The impulse in the diaphragm which caused his laugh returns, but this time the emotion scatters in many directions, and he can feel the nudge of tears and the sting of rage as well.

He's not surprised that Mrs. Grimsden's eyes now burn more sharply than before, and he even sees some colour in her pale cheek. But still, he can't take his stare away, and subtly his body begins to move as though in obedience to some unconscious desire, his back shifting to make his view of her less awkward, his elbow hooking over the back of his chair. Into Mrs. Grimsden's eyes have come real horror now, and if he is not mistaken, some sparks of fear. If he retains his position, he suspects, she will look away soon enough.

He can feel Evelyn's concern trying to distract him, but he's taken control, at least for the moment. Mrs. Grimsden and her plain accusing stare have brought him back to the night where his old life ended and a new one—of scorching dreams and sleepless worries—began. He wonders at his own survival once more, feels the alternative, the icy waters slooping inside his cuffs, rushing up his trouser legs, filling his lungs and belly. How long would death have taken that night? he wonders. Five minutes, perhaps ten. Yet here he is, thirteen years later, still on board the listing deck of the *Titanic,* making his way through the barging crowds to the officers in charge, trying to find order, trying to scrape up hope and reassurance from the chaos. He settles on a moment. He's helping the crew at a lifeboat station, slowly turning a handle of the winch that lowers a lifeboat boat which is only slightly more than half full. His cold-numbed fingers against the metal seem hardly his own. The reality skims through his mind that all of it—the lifeboat swaying from the ropes as it's lowered into the abyss, the winches, davits, the planking under his feet, the great funnels billowing steam, the very handle he turns—are part of *his* plan. The very same pink fingers he sees belong to the hands which inherited from his father the empire of the White Star Line. He and only he, he realizes, can be the architect of whatever disaster he is about to witness.

A petty officer yells across the deck and a cluster of seamen follow his command; he feels the vibrations of their footfalls. Sweet tobacco from a group of gentlemen close to the lounge entrance wafts over him. He catches something of their murmured conversation about Royal Ascot.

Time is suddenly a dreadful thing. He knows it is the sole diminishing barrier between himself crouching at the winch handle overhearing details of horseracing and himself being a central part of a catastrophe so appalling its details are beyond imagination.

The question creeps into his mind for the first time: how much of it dare he witness? He thinks of the ocean, icy enough here in the Labrador current to play host to bergs and growlers, and he thinks of the labyrinth of cabins and corridors already under water below and likely deserted and quiet. The lure is powerful enough to make his hand push too hard.

"Steady there," warns the officer overlooking the lifeboat's descent. Ismay nods and slows down. The faintest sound follows, more *pat* than *splash*. Half a turn more and the lifeboat is freed.

"Father," says Evelyn.

The band ceases, the final high note hanging in the silence. The leader, violin and bow in hand, nods to a scattering of applause. Ismay turns to his daughter, catches her expression, both worried and chiding, and feels a protective layer has been peeled away between them, a taboo breached. He knows it's no use pretending otherwise.

chapter eight

EVELYN ENCOUNTERS *THAT* SMILE, the one he uses with Mother—vague, dithery, sinking into a kind of generalized appeasement. But there's a change in him, too. It was a shock a moment ago to watch him turning to meet the stare of Agnes Grimsden—not necessarily an unwelcome one. It suggests that either he is becoming forgetful and has failed to spot an enemy, or that a fire long doused might be smouldering afresh. He was once a man of authority, and a deeply embedded rock of well-being dwelt under the foundation of their home. Even his fussiness of manner carried an aura, a sense of being associated with work and important matters. When the Ismays went to church and heard about the Almighty from the pulpit, this was the aura Evelyn envisioned, and the picture that went with it was of a carefully waxed moustache, oiled hair, the scent of decision, and the gentleness that would come across such an entity at home after an hour or so with a pipe and playing with the dog.

When he returned Mrs. Grimsden's stare and gave what seemed to be an unforced, disparaging laugh, this almost forgotten father had returned. Evelyn searches his eyes now for some clue to his thoughts.

"Father," she repeats, "are you all right?"

He tilts his head and gives her an affectionate look, lifting his glass.

"Why shouldn't I be all right, my dear?"

Again a tactic used with Mother, and a challenge of a kind. They both know perfectly well why he should be out of sorts. But the cause has never been named and he is banking that their mutual silence will continue. It's a reasonable assumption. Thirteen years of secrecy is like an airtight cell with thick metal walls; the idea of opening it now seems frightening, like scattering a thousand tiny demons into the world.

Not for the first time Evelyn considers that if the memory of the *Titanic* looms over her, and Tom, and Margaret, and Mother, and possibly even George, filling ordinary sounds and objects—a shriek of laughter, the tinkling of wine glasses—with images of catastrophe, how much closer must that terrible event seem to Father? Keeping everything unsaid, even if they all believed it was for Father's good, suddenly seems like a terrible disservice to him. And it all makes so little sense.

Generals who from the safety of distance have knowingly given commands that kill many thousands have then stood proudly with medals pinned to their chests. Yet Father, who hurt no one deliberately, is lambasted publicly, whispered about, stared at, and treated like a pariah. Her anger at them all—the Grimsdens and everyone like them—gives way a little to a sudden rush of admiration for her father, for the fact that he can still sit in a London hotel restaurant, eating, drinking and listening to music; and that when he catches the eye of his accuser, he will stare back and laugh.

Evelyn puts down her knife and fork, hands trembling from pride mingled with fresh indignation. She turns slowly, glimpses Miranda's face bobbing toward her plate, Mr. Grimsden's shoulder, and through a clearing in the foliage, Agnes Grimsden, who has, telepathically, it seems, shifted her own gaze now to her. The look on her face is neither furtive nor unfriendly, but relaxed enough for direct eye contact to suggest communication. For a moment, Evelyn wonders whether she might have it all wrong; perhaps when Mrs. Grimsden had said, "Some men are afraid of everything," she really had been talking about the waiters, and now sees her blunder and is trying to offer some apology and recompense.

As though to confirm this, Mrs. Grimsden tilts her head, raises her eyebrows, and gives a sad, shoulder-heaving sigh, all the while holding Evelyn's gaze. So practiced is Evelyn in the art of pleasing, she begins to find the muscles of her face forming into a smile and the tendons of her neck readying themselves for a nod. But then she remembers Miranda's admission, "There's nothing that can be done with Mother," and the absolute nature of the confirmation that came with it. The power to decipher contradictory messages—the friendly look at her, the insult aimed at her father—comes to Evelyn with a wave of anger. The smile is one of pity; she's showing Evelyn sympathy at having a coward for a father.

She tears her eyes away and counts to three as she looks down at the puckered skin of her pheasant. Picking up her knife and fork again, she glances at Father, who meets her eye straightaway and gives a kindly shrug. But it's no longer enough for either of them, she thinks, not any more.

She wonders if it's too much to hope for that Mrs. Grimsden might need to go to the ladies' cloakroom, whether the attendants there might witness a second drama, one with more lurid details, more escalating conflict, than the first.

Her heart begins to hammer as she realizes such a chance is unlikely. Something truly extreme, and public, is required. She finds it curious suddenly that old-fashioned notions of dignity have remained synonymous with courage. She could remain dignified; it wouldn't be hard. She could avoid the glances of the Grimsdens all evening, sit up straight, sip her wine and talk to Father about all manner of things. But there would be not one ounce of courage in it. Courage is an ugly, red-faced drunkard. Courage leaks spittle and blood. It yells in fury, and causes others to gasp in horror. She remembers witnessing a real argument outside a public house in Liverpool. Two men yelled at each other, their fists clenched, faces deep red, blue veins running down their necks. They seemed scarcely human in their passion, all elbows and boots, angular contraptions designed for conflict. Bobbies waded in before it came to blows, and the crowd, a mix of local gentry and students, who, like Evelyn and her mother, had come from the nearby concert hall, all seemed to give a collective gasp of disapproval.

"Disgraceful display!" she heard a man say.

"Shocking," added someone from another party.

And while Evelyn recognized these were the right things to say, she also realized they were lies, that many of the onlookers were silently captivated, almost admiring, not at the ugliness of it, or the danger, but at the forgetfulness of self, at the sense that these two men were brimming with emotions that were so much bigger than the crowd, so much greater than caution and embarrassment. Evelyn felt a kind of awe bordering on envy. It almost came down to a simple formula, that he who is naked is somehow ennobled, while she who is protected by layer after layer of refinement and manners is diminished, even in a moral sense. *Especially* in a moral sense. Stillness is noble in a flower, not in a human being. To be courageous, to be good, one has to *become* one's emotions, and emotions are seldom dignified.

When she starts to speak, it takes her by surprise. "You're going to have to forgive me, Father." Her lips burn as though her breath is fire. "I'm going to do something."

She looks up and sees him frown, not comprehending, or pretending not to comprehend. Then his pupils contract. "No," he says. There's nothing pleading or fearful in the word. It comes out rather like an order, and again reminds her of the father he once was, kind but in charge.

"It's not just about you anymore," she says. "It's about all of us."

The fork twitches in his hand and an expression of desperate unhappiness comes into his face, hinting at depths of despair she already knows about but has rarely seen. She almost relents. But the anguish seems to pass from him. He lays down his knife and fork, calmly takes a sip of water and coughs slightly as he lowers the glass to the tablecloth.

"And what exactly are you going to do? You can't sue someone for looking at us."

Already Evelyn is shifting in her seat with the urgency of it all. War has been declared, and publicly. "Something, Father," she says. "I have to do something." The blood pounds in her ears, not like something liquid at all, but wooden, muffled and pounding. As children, she and

Margaret used to practice holding pillows over their heads, seeing how long they could go without breathing, and now all those experiments seem like a string of premonitions, bringing her to this point in her life. She wishes the association might provide some clue as to how, precisely, she should act. But it's already too late. She is already standing, putting her napkin on the table, still half wishing for some interruption, another bird perhaps, even a bomb or a man wielding a gun and running amok around the tables.

As luck would have it the palm shields her approach and her nerves become quiet. For all anyone will know, she is merely coming toward the foliage for a better look, to examine the exotic, rubbery leaves; she has seen diners do this on previous occasions and knows it still might provide a reasonable alibi for a tactical retreat. But she catches Miranda's face—her startled eyes, set in a face of patchwork white and pink, an exotic primate chanced upon by an explorer and terrified of being taken captive.

She moves out from the palm and circles toward the Grimsdens' table. Miranda gives an audible gasp and the young man opposite her moves as though preparing to rise, but the energy coming from him is confused. His gaze darts from one face to another and he remains seated. Although the sudden hush is profound, Agnes Grimsden, whom she turns to face, meets her eyes with interest but no apparent fear.

"You seem to have something on your mind, Mrs. Grimsden." The voice Evelyn hears is hardly her own but is, at least, steady, unwavering. "Is there anything you would like to discuss with Father or me?"

"What?" The first interruption, unexpectedly somehow, is from Mr. Grimsden; part word, part cough, and part laugh, it seems unchivalrous, almost bullying, especially delivered from a sitting position.

"Goodness!" says Mrs. Grimsden, smiling, a hand coming to her chest in mock protectiveness.

Evelyn takes a gulp of air, feels the floor grow unsteady beneath her. A young waiter two tables away seems to glare at her as he spoons potatoes from a serving bowl, and there are signs that faces on other tables are turning her way.

"It's quite simple," she says, feeling what's left of her confidence drain as though from an invisible siphon. "I had the distinct impression you were trying to communicate something. I would like to know what it was."

It does sound simple, she tells herself, and reasonable, but her skin is on fire and her vision blurring. The voice she hears has become stiff, yet emotional, and the extraordinary silence that greeted her arrival subsides into tired sighs, one from Mrs. Grimsden, another most likely from her husband; she is too focused upon her target to confirm, too aware that if she lets the challenge of eye contact slip, she will not be able to establish it again.

But in another moment she does let it slip as, dimly, she becomes aware of another problem. Although the hush has lifted from the Grimsden table, a tangible murmur of interest is rippling outwards. A quick glance shows a lady just a few years her senior, with dangling gold earrings, craning her neck and staring at her. The woman whispers to a man at her table, who then raises his head to see. Farther off, toward the restaurant entrance, a mixed party halts their conversation to watch. The air in the restaurant changes—becomes electric with some new interest; a strange young woman standing alone at a table where the menfolk are still seated. The grumble of conversation softens to a murmur, and then fades into a hush, as Evelyn fires another stare into the bemused smile of Agnes Grimsden. She has never been so aware of herself, of how she must look from the outside—a stark, stranded figure with arms stretched rigid at her sides, confronting a woman old enough to be her mother—and the withering shame of it goes through to her bones. She feels movement at her right side, a man standing close to her shoulder, his presence too near for comfort.

"Can I help madam back to her seat?"

As she flinches, she catches enough of a glimpse to know he is the same young waiter who glared at her a few moments ago.

"When I'm ready," she says, expecting his hand to

come down upon her shoulder, shrinking from it in anticipation. She keeps her gaze on the form of Mrs. Grimsden now, on the pearls, the long earrings, the bony shoulders within the onyx-jewelled dress. Her vision slips onto the scattered black jewels themselves, like swirling portholes in an Impressionist's nightmare.

"Ismay." The voice, soft as the wings of a moth, emanates from a few tables distant; the name, Evelyn thinks, seems almost to have been designed for whispering.

There's a fresh wave of murmurs which takes an age to spread to the far reaches of the dining room, where voices seem to resound and echo before returning, like a poorly synchronized communal prayer, converging and rising into a single gasp.

Evelyn becomes aware again of the tautness of her arms. She measures the distance between her right hand and Mrs. Grimsden's face, knows that in a flash she can really give them all something to stare at, that these people are all enemies, every one of them, and that what they think of her and her father can't get any worse. But the helplessness of it all is overpowering and she feels as though she's balancing cannonballs upon both shoulders.

"Evelyn," comes Father's voice to her left. "Let's return to the table." He touches her gently on the left shoulder and her courage returns. She meets Mrs. Grimsden's face squarely once more, sees a glassiness over otherwise triumphant eyes, a touch of a tremble about the lips. Her gaze slips as she turns to Miranda, whose head is down, eyes blinking wildly.

A thought comes to her, makes her throat and tongue itch to free it. It's a mad, extravagant thought that makes her think of barred windows and padded cells, yet only the calming presence of her father as he leads her back to the table stops her from yelling it with all the force of her lungs.

As he pulls out her chair, to the watching silence of the dining room, the impulse becomes smothered—but barely, uncomfortably, like swallowed air. And she regrets this immediately, already wants to hear the shock that would have greeted the words: *It's a pity you weren't all on the* Titanic!

chapter nine

MIRANDA'S SKIN IS ALIVE with pins and needles, and the thought repeats over and over: *it's happened; it's happened.* The words prickle between her toes, dart like flies from her hair to the arcs at the top of her ears, to her shoulders and down the back of her dress.

Father makes an astonished guffawing sound, followed by, "Fancy!" and in a moment, sooner than she might have expected, plates begin to tinkle again near and far with the sound of cutlery. The gentle hum of conversation becomes a buzz. Miranda can feel the interest of Graham, wants to meet his eye and gain comfort from the sympathy his gaze always gives her. But she's afraid to look up, afraid to catch her mother's eye.

It's all her own doing, she knows. Belated as the punishment might be, it's Miranda whose actions unleashed this misery and confusion. She set it in motion with that letter, and kept it brewing again tonight, when she ducked behind the shield of her mother, daring the Ismays to strike.

"What extraordinary behaviour," Mother says after a moment or two. "I really thought the girl was going to hit me! What do you make of it, Miranda?"

Miranda looks up at last, feeling nauseated. She hasn't been picked for an opinion at random. When Mother asks for her thoughts it's always because she's implicated in something.

"I think she was angry," Miranda says quietly, wishing that she could whisk Graham away, tell him all about her childish letter to Mr. Ismay, her own feeling of shame and horror, and all the misery and self-loathing that brought it about in the first place. She wishes she could unburden the whole story before her mother will get to torture her with it. But she knows it's too late, that humiliations will likely unravel, and on her mother's terms, without the context that Mother would neither fully understand, nor wish others to know about.

But it's the context that swallows Miranda now as her hand limply picks up her fork and pushes carrots around on her plate. She's in New York, thirteen years ago. It's a day or so after she cut and pasted the newspaper article. A new superstition, and a fresh sense of mission, rushes in her ears. She's at the desk in the hotel suite's little nursery bedroom, looking beyond the avenue at the rolling foliage in Central Park opposite the road. As the breeze captures the branches, sets the leaves dancing, turning silver in the sunshine, the huge oaks and beeches seem paternal and wise, true guardians of mysteries and insights yet to be unravelled. There are signs in everything, she thinks; nature is sending these visions to her as her father's emissaries. He needs her help just as she needs his.

She crumples the first letter, a simple desperate plea to be rescued, and begins to scratch out another, more veiled in the adult language she has been trying to emulate:

Mister Johnston has been so kind to Mother, they spend all their time together. Everyone here thinks they are man and wife! Somewhere outside in the suite, the bedroom perhaps, Mr. Johnston laughs in his extravagant way—nothing is on an ordinary scale with Mother and Mr. Johnston; it is as though they are playing out some great drama requiring grand gestures and shimmering clothes. Miranda has been hearing cupboard doors opening and closing for some time; Mother and Mr. Johnston are getting ready to go to the theatre, but she knows they can take ages over preparations. Things might easily go quiet again for twenty minutes or more, and then the sound of footsteps and cupboards might begin all over again. They can't leave yet, anyway, as Jenny, who is supposed to mind her, hasn't arrived.

She hears the staccato clop of her mother's tread quite unexpectedly close to her nursery, then the door creaks open. Miranda turns around and drops the pen.

"Miranda dear," Mother says loudly as though she imagined an audience crouching in the shadowed corners of the room. Her eyelids flicker oddly, as though shielding herself from being looked at too directly. "Mr. Johnston is about to escort me to the theatre where we are to meet some friends of mine and your father's. Will you be all right until Jenny arrives to look after you?"

"Yes, Mother." Miranda's face stings with the heat; Mother's dress sways as she goes to leave, but then hesitates.

She bustles in and Miranda turns abruptly back to the desk and leans over the letter so it won't be visible.

"Why so secretive?" laughs Mother uneasily, laying her hand upon Miranda's shoulder. "What's this?"

Miranda goes rigid. Mother eases her backwards with surprising strength so that her forearms slide from the letter, leaving it exposed. In the silence, Miranda's vision blurs. Beneath the urgent fear and shame flutters a wisp of a true desire, that her reasons for acting as she does be understood, that her mother see the loneliness, the confusion, and the fear. But it's a feather before a tidal wave; she knows what is coming. Before she has had time to brace herself, she feels the blow, the sting of her cheek, the sudden deafness in her right ear followed by a clear, high note.

"I don't understand you!" Mother whispers savagely. Miranda catches the scent of her lipstick and perfume as

Mother pulls away the letter and crumples it. "I'll never understand you! Do you want it all to end? Do you? Do you want your father to leave us? Do you want to live on the street? Is that what you want?"

Miranda's been breathing hard, keeping closed upon herself like a hedgehog under attack. Now her mother turns and strides away, she feels the tug, as though she's connected to her mother by a rope attached around her waist. She feels the tears now rolling down her cheeks and creeping into her mouth, and miraculously almost, Mother turns.

"It's that ship," she says softly kneading the crumpled letter in her fingers as she speaks, "that dreadful voyage has upset us all. I'm sorry, Miranda. We'll spend the day tomorrow, just the two of us."

MOTHER'S GAZE REMAINS ON her, amused and questioning. The palm between their table and the Ismays seems to shiver. Miranda's eyes dart in that direction, half expecting a second attack from Evelyn, but her view has returned to the way it was when she first glanced at Mr. Ismay. Again it's that face bordered by an irregular star-shaped gap in the foliage, his face concerned, glassy-eyed, intent upon his companion as he raises his fork to his lips.

"I could see she was angry, Miranda dear. I was wondering if you had any other profound insight." Her voice has taken on that odd sing-song quality that confuses newcomers to the Grimsden family, like poor Graham. Miranda, however, knows it to indicate a sense of dissatisfaction, of not being sufficiently entertained by the people with whom she sits. It is the voice of fading grandeur bemoaning the present lack of ebullience, the inability to see the dramatic potential in any given situation.

Miranda winces, and this time beneath her distaste for her mother she feels the stirring of an anger that rather scares her. She has so far treated this evening as an exercise in controlling others but feels suddenly, like an object turning in the water to reveal contours unsuspected, she may end up trying to control herself.

"No, Mother," she replies plainly, almost sulkily. "I don't have any profound insight beyond the obvious fact that she doesn't like her father to be talked about in a negative fashion." Her mother's eyes narrow, seeing the challenge, but still Miranda continues. "But that dreadful voyage upset us all, didn't it, Mother?"

This is the closest she has come in many years to bringing up the *Titanic* herself and alluding to her own conduct, the letter she wrote to Mr. Ismay. It's thrilling, somehow, as well as terrifying, the idea that her own personal taboo may be slipping. She feels its incredible weight through its sudden absence. So many afternoons and evenings she has spent in company with Mother flirting around the subject of Miranda and the *Titanic*—her daughter's strong belief in courage and cowardice, some action connected with that belief—teasing forth the topic with allusions subtle or daring, then moving the conversation abruptly away if a direct question is asked. Always the guardian against her daughter's pain, she then gives Miranda her sympathetic look—the code a reminder for the secret bond they share.

Now she's come close to broaching the subject herself, Miranda feels her shoulders and neck muscles loosening. It's no more than a taste of liberty, a slight dent in an oppression sustained for so long, since September 1912, a day after she sent the letter. Her imagination spins on the thread of that memory now, the blood-thumping panic as Miranda read those words—*libel, lawsuit, ruination*—in one of Father's newspapers. She'd been asked to fetch it from the study, had been holding the broad sheets one way, then another, unable to get the creases right, the way Father liked it, when the words first caught her attention and hauled her into the story of a businessman now claiming bankruptcy.

She stood there in the dim light, the hanging page making a hushing sound against the leather of Father's chair, as she delved further into the world of adulthood she had entered stealthily the day before. She had an idea those three words might also be connected in some unforeseeable way with her own communication to Mr. Ismay, but the rush of terror was at first slow to come. She read a few lines and creaked slowly toward the door, laid the newspaper upon the carpet, planning to fold it again properly, but read a little more, enough to realize that libel occurred when one person said something bad against another, and that ruination—*financial* ruination—would come down upon the person who had spoken ill.

Father lived in dread of financial ruination. It had occurred to some of his friends, and to Uncle John, and as far as Miranda could tell, he arranged everything in his life as a dam against any possibility of it occurring to him. And without him knowing, she had already set this disaster in motion; the letter was on its way and she already knew enough of schoolgirl pranks gone wrong to realize she could not prevent its delivery. Frantic now with fear, Miranda folded the newspaper inside out so that the football scores were on the crumpled outside. She rushed into the sitting room, handed the sheath to Father, who took it in surprise and laughed, then shot out of the sitting room and into the hallway, flying up the stairs two at a time.

Mother was silent at the mirror when Miranda entered, her breathing too urgent for words. When she did manage to speak through gulps for air, what she said made little sense to Mother or to herself. The confusion in her mother's eyes deepened into interest when she managed to talk about the letter she had written, and then softened into the warmth of a confidence between them when she at last connected the whole episode to her fears of reprisals in the courts.

"You were right to send the letter, Miranda," she'd said soothingly, when she had drawn most of the content from her daughter. "Mr. Ismay is a coward and you were brave to challenge him." She had sat Miranda down upon her bed, and with a sense of privilege and luxury, Miranda watched as her mother dressed herself for the evening. They had a housekeeper and a maid and Mother had often talked of a personal maid to help her dress, had always rather disparaged her father for the fact they were without one. But Miranda was terribly happy there was no one between the two of them as Mother's underskirts rustled between the wardrobe and the bed, as straps were fastened and fabric smoothed. It all told Miranda that what she had done, and who she was, matched an ideal she carried in her head. "Don't worry, Miranda dear," Mother said, applying her lipstick. "He'll never dare show it, because it's true. But don't tell your father anyway. He's a worrier. All men are. It'll be our secret."

"I KNOW IT ALL upset *you*, Miranda," Mother says. A quality appears in Mother's eyes that Miranda doesn't recognize—something fluid and wavering. She guesses at once that it must be fear.

"I did things I was ashamed of, yes," Miranda replies.

The wavering in Mother's eyes intensifies. If she was afraid a moment ago, Miranda thinks, this could only be alarm. There was an unspoken second part to the statement, a symmetry left incomplete. I did things I was ashamed of, yes, and so did you. Though oblivious of all the meanings, Graham and Father have noticed something too. Graham looks between Miranda and Mother, his glance furtive and worried. Father coughs and looks directly at his wife, which he hardly ever does, searching for some clue. They can all feel it under their feet, Miranda thinks, a sudden imbalance, something dangerous that may at any moment tip into confusion and ruin.

The realization is swift and, once achieved, infuriatingly obvious. It wasn't accident or fate, or a psychological quirk of Miranda's which chained her so decisively to her own past actions. Mother forged those chains, deliberately, knowingly, because behind it all there was something altogether more pernicious, the memory of laughter and sudden silence in a hotel suite, the creaking of a bed past midnight. Now Miranda has disowned her shackles and they have fallen, at least for the moment, and Mother is panicking. They can all see that, even Graham, although Father and he can hardly know the reason. And Mother in a panic is terrifying because hers is the force that somehow keeps them all afloat.

chapter ten

ISMAY FEELS HIS DAUGHTER'S agony as though it were a fire burning him from the inside. The look, pleading and helpless, she gave him when he escorted her back to the table has remained, but now it's directed away from any human including himself.

"Sorry," she merely said to him as he took his seat opposite.

"It doesn't matter." He shrugged, almost light-heartedly and meaning it for once. He *could* be carefree if it would help her; it was a small enough price to pay for her loyalty and love, and the people here would fade in importance the moment they left the building. But so great was the weight piled upon that single word of apology, Ismay was unable to prise her out from beneath it.

"You know, Evelyn," he says, watching her lift her fork and lay it down again. "Most of us try to get through life without being compromised, without ever being embarrassed, which is an extraordinary thing if you think about it, when there is so much war, so many disasters and tragedies, real and man-made." He doesn't know where he's going with this speech, hears it as a listener would hear it, without foreknowledge but with a vague sense of its sincerity. "What you did just now is, in the eyes of the world to which we belong, the worst kind of crime. But I find it profoundly touching and I am very grateful."

She looks up at last and gives him a sad smile.

As though to illustrate the point of her crime, a stern-faced waiter hovers behind her.

"Madam is finished?" he asks, white-gloved hand reaching for her plate.

"I think not," Ismay says.

"Yes, I'm finished," says Evelyn, and the waiter snaps up her plate and circles to Ismay's side of the table. The wine waiter converges upon them and swiftly fills their glasses. The urgency around their table draws fresh glances.

Evelyn sighs as she turns to meet some of these faces, and they look away quickly enough. Ismay is glad to see a return of her sparkle.

"When will they stop trying to make you pay for it?" she says.

"Never." He lifts his glass, tips it in a mock toast and sips. "But I did make that choice."

"Now you sound like one of them." She presses her fingertips to her glass stem.

One of the waiters, the more surly of the two, has taken a position close to their table, a yard or two behind Evelyn. He stares straight ahead, and Ismay realizes there is a strategy afoot to press them into an early exit. An improbable rebellion bristles on the back of his neck. He feels a sudden urge to frustrate their plans.

"I say, waiter," he calls. The man's eyes grow alarmed and it seems for a moment he plans to pretend he hasn't heard. Then, as though following direction from someone behind Ismay, he nods and approaches the table. He bends, with his ear close to Ismay like a conspirator. "We'd like to see the dessert menu, please."

The waiter, still with ear close to Ismay's mouth, makes a low sound as though considering how to respond. He raises himself a little and shuffles backwards, aiming his own comments somewhere just behind Ismay's head.

"But, sir, we wondered whether you and madam wouldn't be more comfortable in your suite."

"No, we would not," Ismay says.

He sees that Evelyn is beginning to shift, and already has her gloves on the table. He throws her a slight frown to make her stop.

"But as you can see, sir, we are very busy."

"And as you can see, we have not finished."

The waiter moves away without another word and Evelyn obediently folds away her gloves.

Ismay catches a glance or two from adjacent tables.

The band returns, and he wonders at the shortness of the break, whether they've been instructed to recommence to smooth over the unpleasantness between Evelyn and the Grimsdens. The leader waves his violin bow like a conductor's stick and they strike into a mid-tempo waltz Ismay doesn't immediately recognize. It's not "The Blue Danube" but something quite similar.

"We're both misbehaving tonight, aren't we, Father?"

"Well, you know, one may as well be hung for a sheep."

The image, ironically, makes him think of the ocean, perhaps because it evokes notions of courage and manhood, perhaps because it's accompanied by a waltz that feels like the motion of waves. He's bent at the winch handle once more, hearing the *pat* and *splash* as the lifeboat touches down upon the water's surface more than sixty feet below. In a moment more the lifeboat is freed and he's racing with some other sailors to launch one of the two collapsibles stored upon the boat deck.

Sounds of distant panic rise and fade, but mostly there is an unreal sense of quiet and order even in the rush. It's a stomach-heaving calm because he knows it can't possibly last. Soon there will be panic and agony beyond anything he has ever imagined. Life doesn't depart peacefully, even if it is one life trapped within the body of one long-ailing. This will not be one, or ten, or a hundred, and those to die are not ailing. They are merely aboard a ship that cannot remain above the surface of the water.

Ropes are slung aside with a slap. Ismay helps throw them clear. Carter, the friendly Philadelphian chap, appears at his shoulder and throws him a sympathetic look that makes Ismay wonder. On the one hand, there's hardly time to consider everything, on the other, there are oceans of time. Every moment lasts forever. As a seaman reaches his long spanner to a nut high on the davit and turns it with a grunt, it seems that—in that swift glance—Carter, a recent acquaintance, has suddenly acquired the ability to read his thoughts. It feels as though he knows Ismay is thinking of the decks below and the peace that likely reigns in that place now that all the life of the ship must have swarmed upwards. Boiler rooms, post rooms, swimming pools, steerage, and many cabins aft will be submerged and silent. His kingdom. The urge to go down there tugs him so hard he almost feels himself dissolve into the darkness between the cabin lights, making his escape from the scene in a trail of vapour.

Carter catches his eye for a second time as collapsible boat C shifts from its blocks with a yelp. Chief Officer Wilde hands a lantern to a seaman on the far side and he places it inside the lifeboat hull. The lifeboat sways from its ropes as it hangs precariously from the deck. All the boats so far have made it down, but this seems altogether harder. The list is now so pronounced the lifeboat will have trouble balancing from the ropes and could easily scud against the side and tip over.

"Women and children first," Wilde shouts. Two or three seamen join the first inside and get ready to receive. There's a pause from the huddled grey clump of third-class passengers, then at last the bustle of movement, white funnels of breath, maybe two dozen or so women in coats and several children, like young deer among a herd, confused, quiet and moist-eyed. Shoes clatter on hollow planking and the suspended lifeboat sways ominously, davits creaking. A last circle of five or six women and a few men stand on the deck, unwilling to commit.

"How many for this boat, Mr. Wilde?" Ismay shouts. He means to urge the undecided forward.

"Yes, more." He waves his hand to encourage them on. They go silently, gripping one another's sleeves to keep balanced. Hands reach out from the darkness of the lifeboat hull, guiding the newcomers to a place.

"Lower away," he says. The davit creaks violently. The rim of the lifeboat bumps hard against the ship's side. The winches this time are turned by seamen and Ismay feels suddenly weightless on the deck, a man of no substance whose avowed purpose is grinding to a halt. He eases a half-step away, feeling Carter's attention on him again, knowing that if he is to disappear and go below, this is the time—the catastrophe is closing upon them all.

"You have a wife and children, don't you, Ismay?"

The voice is disembodied, emerging from a silence and

calm somewhere beyond the creaking of the davit and the winch.

Ismay watches the heads jiggling upon shoulders as the boat jerks slightly lower.

"Yes."

He turns to catch Carter's slightly bemused smile.

"Stop," Wilde calls. The men at the winches halt. "Steady, a quarter turn." Wilde gestures to the man at the bow side. The lifeboat sways and evens up a little.

Silence is suddenly profound. Ismay turns to see the bareness of the deck and the steepness of its incline. In a few more minutes he will have to hold onto a railing merely to stand. The sound of distant thumps, rattles, and crashes punctuate the hush. And he knows the noise will increase like an orchestra tuning up before a performance. He knows it will reach a cacophony, and that agony and death will surely follow, on the ship, in the water, in the lifeboats, perhaps, should the sinking ship carry them under, should the sea become choppy, should the racing *Carpathia* not find them. And that this will only be the beginning.

The shock will carry over the airwaves. The staccato beat of wireless will transmit the news via Cape Race: that one of the largest steamships in the world has been swallowed whole by the glassy Atlantic; that the sinking was slow enough to provide for an evacuation of the passengers by lifeboats.

How long will it take them to fill in the rest of the

story, that the lifeboats could hold far fewer than half the two thousand or so on board? The early optimism will make the blow of reality harsher. The true horror of it will unfold through agonizing, incremental stages. Printed news of the sinking might appear as early as the morning in New York, in the late editions in London. The first editorials will quiver with uncertainty, but press the need for calm. But after the lifeboats are reached—please God—the survivors counted, the news will likely change. A catastrophe becomes real only when news of it is communicated. This one will come to life with the dailies, the phone calls, and the urgent worry of it all.

The relatives of passengers, of officers and men, stewards, stewardesses, valets, cooks, and staff will gather at notice boards outside the Southampton office, the New York office, the London office. Reporters will mill among the grief-stricken. His own—his Julia, Tom, Margaret, Evelyn, and George—will huddle at home, awaiting the phone call or wire.

But none of it has happened yet, so none of it is real. If he skips away now, if he weaves downwards into the ship away from the familiar, through steerage, into the bowels, he will be able to un-imagine it all. He will die as Thomas Ismay's son and heir, a man always destined to out-build his father. He will exit the world a success. The new world, the one of agonizing pain and unmitigated disaster, will be forever unborn.

Something breaks the quiet, no more than a murmur really, from the jerking collapsible C, but he catches the words.

"Someone will have to pay, that's for sure."

He finds himself nodding silently in agreement, as though he were a passenger, quite outside his own clothes. Recompense does indeed follow a tragedy that has been inflicted by human agency. Hard-earned money paid everyone's passage on this magnificent ship, whether it is the first-class industrialist's family, the second-class headmaster, or the humble steerage passenger hoping to build a life as a fruit farmer somewhere in the great American interior. They gave the White Star Line their money and their trust. In the tipping deck, the violently creaking davits, in the distant thunder of falling lamps and tables, he feels injustice and betrayal just as they do. There's something comforting in the truism: someone will have to pay; it's solid and reliable like the ground beneath one's feet when all else is scattered.

It takes a while, though less than a second perhaps, for Ismay to realize that the "someone" referred to can only be him. The speaker, whose face now drops almost level with the deck, didn't know that, of course; she likely doesn't know who he is, yet it mars the oblivion of which he's been dreaming. His father built ships and so did he. But everything has changed. He remembers the image of St. Sebastian from his Religious Studies school book, the tortured face and the dozen or so fiery arrows burning into his skinny flesh. This is the future beyond this moment should he choose to live through it. He must pay.

"Hold it!" cries Wilde to one of the seamen. "Slower your end. Wait, wait, crank it back an inch and start again."

The lifeboat rim thumps against the hull again and seamen inside push carefully with the paddle end of their oars to keep it clear.

"Well, Ismay?" says Carter. "What about it? There's no one else on deck."

Has the man been reading my thoughts again? Ismay wonders. Carter lifts his hands, palms out, as though to signal futility, then with the careless ease and balance of an athlete steps onto the boat.

"Trouble, Mr. Wilde?" asks First Officer Murdoch. Ismay hadn't noticed him approach and wonders now whether Murdoch is making reference to Carter, who is now seated.

"We're trying to keep it clear, sir; we'll have it in a moment."

A single oar paddle keeps the lifeboat rim several inches clear.

"All right. Hold it steady a second."

Wilde and Murdoch both turn and look expectantly at Ismay.

The decision, Ismay realizes, is made. It's just a question of making his limbs obey. Spider-like, they do, as he clambers quietly aboard. Carter's hand comes under his arm. Someone else shifts to the side.

"Lower away," comes the order.

"MILES AWAY AGAIN, FATHER?"

"Yes, miles away."

It's a radical change, that he should admit it, and so effortlessly. Evelyn smiles, and a kind of comfort settles over them. The acceptance of it all—that he is the "villain" who stepped onto the lifeboat, that she is the furious young woman who has caused their near ejection from the restaurant—seems like a balm. What else can touch them now, after all? Even the frantic energy with which the surly young waiter hands the dessert menu first to Evelyn, then to Ismay, can't quite dispel it. The man stands, hands behind his back, to the rear of Ismay's chair.

"Take your time, Evelyn dear," Ismay says.

As his eyes skim the offerings, everything from French cuisine desserts—crème brûlée, meringues, crêpe suzette to English staples such as roly-poly pudding and spotted dick—he feels the letters merge before his eyes like a swarm of flies, scatter and reform into a different kind of list, a series of possible actions—*go to the Grimsden table, confront them yourself; confront Mr. Grimsden, my obvious counterpart, make him either apologize or pay for the insolence of his wife, the accepted chivalrous thing to do; sit down with them without an invitation, act as though they are your friends and gently begin to lace pleasantries with challenges and insinuations.*

Each idea makes his heart pick up speed and his blood gather urgency. The thing he was most afraid of, that his children would be drawn into a battle to defend his honour, really has occurred. The ship is sinking, and there is no face left to lose.

chapter eleven

"WHAT IS THE MATTER, Agnes?" Father asks with some impatience. His frown looks like anger but Miranda knows it is worry. Like a marionette with too few strings, he only has one "unhappy" expression, a deepening of furrows on his forehead and a sharpening of the eyes.

Mother hauls her gaze from Miranda. "Nothing, my dear," she says, and Miranda notices a slight tremor in her earrings. "It's just strange the things people find to be ashamed of, isn't it?"

Father and Graham look even more puzzled than before, and Miranda, for the first time, sees properly the essential weakness in Mother's extroversion. When she is in command, as she is most of the time, everything goes smoothly. She dominates the conversation, dictates changes in subject, and decides who should be in the spotlight and—when mood decides—who should squirm.

But when she loses control, as she has now, she can't stop talking, and her words lay her open and exposed.

"What do you mean, Mother?" asks Miranda.

Even if cruelty, the certain knowledge that her mother can't answer without tying herself in knots, lurks behind the question, Miranda is also prompted by the anxiety she sees in the face before her. She still half means to rescue her mother, to prevent the spilling of something worse than cryptic comments, something related to her own sleeping guilt.

Mother throws her a glance and Miranda wonders whether she sees pleading or defiance. "I mean," Mother says, with hardly a pause, "that here we are, years after that terrible event, years after men of privilege and rank saved themselves while honest humble folk perished, women, men, and children hoping for a life in the new world. And somehow," she looks up at Graham for a moment, lips tightening, fingers holding the stem of her glass, "I'm the one who's causing the trouble."

This is too much, Miranda thinks, a secondhand opinion grasped at because, in the miasma of Mother's brain, it happens to float into view. But switching personalities has always been one of Mother's chief tactics; if nothing else, it keeps the enemy confused. Miranda's face burns with anger at the slipperiness of her mother, who, she is certain, will never lose an argument.

"I had no idea, Mother," she says, "no idea at all that

your arguments against Mr. Ismay were socialist in nature." Miranda sees Graham wince, knows he thinks she has gone too far, but rather like Mother herself, she doesn't quite know how to stop. "I believe you'll find you have much in common with Mr. H. G. Wells on the subject, and Mr. George Bernard Shaw. But it's quite a revelation that you feel that way."

"Miranda," Graham chides under his breath, but loud enough for Mother to hear. Miranda feels her confidence drain and a new heat prickling under her skin. However reticent Graham has been, she's had the belief, always, that he was on her side. This declaration proves this is not the case. And the effect of it on Mother is obvious. She seems calmer straightaway, and the imperious air begins to return.

"In acting as he did," she says determinedly, "in getting into a lifeboat before women and children, Ismay conceded the very ground upon which our society is founded. He threw it all to the Bolsheviks, to Mr. Wells and Mr. Shaw. He showed that the system of leadership and nobility we all adhere to is a lie."

Mother's point is made with such quiet conviction and to such impressive silence that it takes a moment for Miranda to notice the glaring contradiction.

"So *is* it a lie, Mother?"

"No! Of course not! He made it seem so."

"I see," says Miranda, half-defeated. She can't argue

with them all now Graham has shown his hand. Graham merely wants peace, clearly, and will back the speaker whose victory will dampen the conflict. He's astute enough to know that this could only be his prospective mother-in-law. Father has returned from concern to his habitual detachment. His brown eyes gaze upon his wife in a vague, relieved kind of way.

Miranda looks at Graham, willing direct eye contact, hoping for the chance to give him some hint as to the depth of his blunder. But he looks altogether too comfortable, even gives a little grin as he takes a sip of wine and glances from prospective father-in-law, to prospective mother-in-law, to Miranda—as if to convey that such disagreements among family members are rather jolly really, part of the rough and tumble, and that he looks forward to more of it. Meanwhile the feeling of having been betrayed simmers under Miranda's skin; already, words like "traitor" and "coward" form on her tongue. She knows herself well enough to understand this feeling, stifled, will only grow as the seconds and minutes tick away. Graham's *"Miranda!"* though nothing but a small tug at the time, a slight tremor through the course of her argument with Mother, will echo louder and louder until, alone together in Graham's flat after the meal, she will be spitting fury at him.

She feels a sweaty discomfort under her engagement ring. Hands under the table, she loosens the band, twists it off, then, lifting the purse strap from the chair behind her, makes sure that Graham, to her right, catches sight of her opening the purse and dropping the ring inside.

"Too tight?" asks Graham mildly.

"Pretty uncomfortable tonight, yes."

"We'll have to see about it."

"Yes," she says curtly and tries to catch his eye again, but Mother, who has been off on a brief reverie of her own, captures his attention first.

"We've lost sight of what was important once," she says, her voice tragic and theatrical, her eyes seemingly deeper set than usual. "The concepts that held our world together have fallen away."

"Honour and chivalry and all that?" says Graham. Suddenly he seems like a young pack animal, all quivering whiskers and wagging tail, trying to gain acceptance.

"And decency, yes. Dying words, I'm afraid."

She sees Father check his watch and she feels impatient for the evening to end, feels impatient to get to Graham. Her anger frees her to take a glance beyond the palm, where she has noticed some activity. Her distaste for Mother and her disgust with Graham make her feel like switching clans, moving over once more to the enemy of her enemy. Mr. Ismay, happier and more relaxed than he has looked all evening, holds up a menu and talks to a rather morose waiter, the same one who seems to have been shadowing their table since the incident. She's been aware of the waiter's uniform, a blur of black and white in the corner of her eye. For a while he stood statue-like in a spot close to the Ismay table, and then she noticed him leave and come back with menus, rooting himself once more. At first she believed the Ismays were going to be asked to leave. It doesn't seem that way now, although the waiter's moustache twitches uncomfortably while he takes the order.

She turns to see her mother's steadfast gaze. It burns her a little, this mini confrontation across the table, and Miranda realizes that if Graham has been disloyal to her, then no doubt in her mother's mind, Miranda has been disloyal to Mother with her *I did things I was ashamed of, yes*, and its unspoken codicil, albeit one only Mother would understand. But perhaps in the world of the Grimsdens this was enough. Alluding to a past misconduct in a public setting, with the implied threat it *could* be made public, was as bad as an outright betrayal. All this she has learned from the woman who stares across at her. The thought causes an unbearable, suffocating feeling to swell up inside her, together with the fear that she'll never be free because all these tactics, and codes, and subterfuges are *inside* her. And the battle, the constant stress of it, uses up all her energy. She could have spent her strength tonight on apologizing properly to the Ismays, on trying to put things as right as she could. But that would have been too straightforward, too open and too easy. Instead she's wasted her time and efforts on doing battle with her mother.

She recalls the talk after the disaster, of a man being shot dead by an officer because he tried to clamber aboard a lifeboat, of older boys being hauled up from under the skirts of women and back onto the deck. She didn't witness any of this, but it was a huge ship and she has no reason to doubt that it happened. And sometimes it's as if, by magic, she and her mother have been caught ever since in that same repeating loop of behaviour. They, like the officers on board the *Titanic*, have spent their time and efforts preventing progress. Officers fired pistols, raved, and yelled to keep the "wrong" people off the lifeboats—some of which left the ship less than half full; Mother and Miranda scheme and strategize against each other, defending their ground from intrusion, when specific goals are left unattained.

Mother looks away at last, stifling a little yawn that might be put on, and peruses diners at other tables. Following her gaze to a table where an elderly lady fans herself, Miranda feels a lightning rod of memory, a restless crowd, the constant moth-like movement of fans, summer in New York under the high ceiling in New York's Natural History Museum.

Shoe heels echo along the hard floor and Miranda scampers to keep up with Mother, always a fast walker. Mother receives Miranda's hand and they slow down and turn together to view the next exhibit.

"Doesn't it put everything into perspective, Miranda, being here?"

Mother smiles at Miranda, squeezes her hand, and both of them look up at the shiny, dark reconstructed skeleton of a woolly mammoth. This is the day after the argument about the letter to Father, a day with just the two of them, an apology of sorts, and a warm buzz of euphoria lives in Miranda's chest.

"Yes, Mummy."

"To think of the cold and inhospitable climates, the savagery and the selfishness from which we have come."

She squeezes her mother's hand in response. She loves to hear Mother talk, though she seldom understands. There's sparkle and poetry in her voice, a kind of romance and a kind of belief.

"And think about the way it was on that terrible night on the Atlantic. Think beyond the cowardice of people like Mr. Ismay, to the heroic captain going down with his ship, the naval architect Mr. Andrews and the many officers and passengers who set their own safety aside."

Miranda stares through the great shadowy holes in the mammoth's skull within which an oversized brain once pulsed with thoughts. Her hand twitches inside her mother's as she struggles to understand the connection between the great fossil before her and the behaviour of people on board the *Titanic* but, nonetheless, she gratefully follows her mother's words.

"Selflessness and sacrifice are true measures of nobility. But it takes many centuries of lessons learned and battles fought. You will learn this too, especially when you have a child of your own. Sacrifice is not always about physical danger. Father had to sacrifice us this summer. He couldn't get away from work. I have to sacrifice, too." She pauses and Miranda feels a weight in the silence, something about to descend. "We are his ambassadors here in America. Mr. Johnston is a delightful man and a friend of the family. He also has relatives who can help your father with his business, and so discretion is very important to us all. Do you know what discretion is, Miranda?"

"Keeping silent," Miranda says.

"Not speaking harm," Mother corrects her gently. She crouches down and takes both of Miranda's hands. "Life is a complicated thing, Miranda." Mother's sweet breath, lipstick mingling with perfume, captivates Miranda; it's the scent of adulthood, a distant promised land. "My father was not as successful as yours, even though he worked hard, terribly hard, all his life. He studied and toiled but it wasn't enough for him. He learned that it can't all be done in a single lifetime. It takes much longer than that, and it can't be done without help. Your father works terribly hard too. He's taken risks that have turned out well for him, but it's a worry for him and a strain. Men like your father need help, but they don't know how to ask for it. That's my job, Miranda. One day it will be your job too."

Miranda nods, a fresh kind of excitement in her belly. She's always been in awe of her mother, who commands respect and devotion wherever she goes. Even though she hates Mr. Johnston always being at the hotel, she is still warmed and reassured by the sheer power of her mother, the way she exuded certainty and safety even upon the freezing lifeboat, the way she drew people to her as soon as they arrived in New York, made their lack of clothes and belongings seem like a game as they juggled gifts, and credit, and money cabled from Father.

Mother holds the magic of the future in her palm. Miranda has been admitted early into this world of confidence and daring, sees marvellous light and rather terrifying dangers. Her mother thinks she is almost ready for these, and the idea is exhilarating.

NOW, JUST MOMENTS AFTER her accusing look, Mother seems old. Disillusionment haunts her eyes as she scans the tables. Miranda can almost see the weight of the years coming down on her, loosening her skin, draining her lips of colour and life. She feels a sudden urge to apologize but knows this is as much of a trap as the desire to argue; it would be another subversion of any genuine goal. And there is nothing specific for which she can legitimately apologize, except perhaps making Mother, rather than herself, into a target for Evelyn Ismay.

The thought takes hold immediately, sending down roots

and sprouting leaves which delineate shapes of possible sentences should she have the courage to broach the subject. It's Father, rather than Graham or Mother, who makes her shy away from merely opening her mouth and talking. There is such a tradition of protecting Father, or protecting herself from his judgment; the two concerns sound like polar opposites but mysteriously merge into the same general dread of creating discomfort or embarrassment for him. She doesn't for the moment know how to get past it.

Father catches her eye as she gazes at him and a premonition of that discomfort sweeps across his face. He sighs and glances at his watch. "You'll have to excuse me, ladies, Graham, for a few moments. I have to go to the lobby and make a phone call."

With a gasp at the serendipity of it, Miranda watches him as he stands, takes a little mock bow and leaves the table. She catches a movement from beyond the palm, a face, Mr. Ismay's, watching him depart. It surprises Miranda, this interest in her father. She had imagined Mr. Ismay to be beyond noticing somehow. She holds onto the thought, as she wants to delay. Now there's nothing between Miranda and her admission, and she sees the icy waters of danger rippling below her, daring her to dive. And this time she must.

"I must apologize to you, Mother," she says abruptly.

Her mother looks startled, worried, her deep-set eyes seem puffy and tired.

"I'm the reason Evelyn Grimsden came to our table."

She feels Graham's astonishment too, can see, without looking, his face has turned the same shade of pink it does after he's been playing rugby.

"You see, I apologized for a letter I once wrote to her father. And it seems to have stirred it all up for her."

"What did you do that for?" The tone in her voice, one of exasperation, suggests she might well have added *you stupid girl*, and probably would have done had Graham not been sitting between them.

"When?" asks Graham, always a stickler for irrelevant details.

"I wrote the letter when I was ten years old, Graham," she says, rather pleased that his prosaic presence lends the scene some stability, that Mother and she will have a certain obligation to remain logical and measured, if only for appearance's sake. "And I apologized to Evelyn in the ladies' room tonight."

"What was in the letter?" asks Graham, and again Miranda is grateful he's there, an interpreter between two long-warring tribes.

"A series of accusations, of cowardice and treachery, a second-hand, childish repetition of all the silliest things that had already appeared in the newspaper." Her ears have gone numb. She looks from Mother's rather disgusted, contemptuous face, to Graham, whose eyelids flutter in urgent embarrassment.

"You were a child," he says.

"An unhappy child, yes. As Mother said, the *Titanic* and everything about it seemed to unhinge us all, rather. I was angry then, and there was nowhere for the anger to go. So I directed it at Mr. Ismay. He seemed such an easy target. In any case, Mother, I apologize. It was I who brought on the attack tonight. Again, sorry."

She stumbled briefly before mentioning her anger. The merest possibility existed that Graham just might ask why she was angry. But then Graham rarely asked open-ended questions. He preferred conversations which narrowed to single points of fact.

"What a luxury it must be to apologize," says Mother.

The comment, glibly thrown, seems at first like another of Mother's fogging tactics; it doesn't mean anything, she thinks, but it prevents anyone from settling into a point of view. It merges with the memory of the museum, the darkened orbs of the mammoth skeleton, the suggestion of ferocious work and sacrifice behind the evolution of the family toward present success. This time, Mother's words really do point to a philosophical difference between Miranda and herself, and one that could only make Miranda seem terribly spoilt, a child whose privilege has been toiled for by others.

She catches a movement from beyond the palm. Mr. Ismay stands. She assumes at first the Ismays are about to leave after all. But Evelyn, as far as she can tell from beyond the leaves, remains seated. Mr. Ismay talks to his daughter for a few moments, his face smiling, his gestures casual, almost frivolous. Then he turns and strides through the dining room into the lobby, oblivious it seems of the faces that glance up from the tables, the whispering conversations left in his wake. Miranda feels a tug in her diaphragm, a sudden frustrated desire to follow. It can't be coincidence that Mr. Ismay should go in the same direction as Father. Waves of panic and defeat move inside her, making her nauseated. She can't begin to imagine what Mr. Ismay and her father will say to each other, or rather what they will do, as a whole new catalogue of dangers opens when men set themselves to battle each other.

She turns back to the palm. A clearing between leaves this time reveals Evelyn's face, her expression blank and pale. Their eyes meet, unhappily. Miranda sees the trace of a nod.

chapter twelve

THREE CONNECTED TELEPHONE BOOTHS stand along the lobby wall. Two are clearly free. Through the bright glass in the middle box, Ismay sees Grimsden, his shoulders hunched, his head bowed, and eyes safely away from the glass. The blue-liveried attendant has already seen Ismay's interest in the phones and opens wide the door to Grimsden's right. Ismay steps inside because he can think of no other way to act. He nods belatedly as the attendant eases the door closed behind him.

He picks up the earpiece with one hand, keeping the holding device depressed with the other. Turning to the lobby he sees the attendant, square-shouldered, gloved hands behind his back, obscuring the view passing hotel staff and guests might get of him through the glass. His face burns with the furtiveness of it all. This is not at all what he envisioned when he followed Grimsden. Ismay had seen his way clear to an honest statement of fact, something to the effect that he did not appreciate Grimsden's wife staring at him and his daughter through dinner, adding perhaps that he is proud of Evelyn's justified challenge. What Grimsden chose to do about it would be his business. All this played out in an obligingly empty corridor without the complication of telephones or hotel staff.

He might have known it wouldn't be this way. Some romantic impulse, brought into being by Evelyn, has given him the notion that tonight rules may be broken. Yet Evelyn herself paid a heavy price in embarrassment and shame for doing so, and Ismay knows he's incapable of diving with such complete abandon into chaos. He doesn't mind a simple argument with Grimsden or anyone else, but has no stomach for the crashing lack of taste that would allow a scene to play out with hotel employees as horrified witnesses, their white-gloved hands attempting to intervene. Perhaps a newspaper reporter might chance upon the disagreement, or be alerted by some passerby, and the full weight of the catastrophe would return in all its horrid hues. He and his family would see it all unravel under some new ignominious headline: *Disgraced Titanic Owner in Public Brawl.*

His life, he realizes, must have always been under a microscope, even before the *Titanic*. Like everyone in his class and position he has always been an ant under the lens, but since there was so little notoriety in his behaviour, the public eyes which glanced upon him—office and hotel employees, railway porters, hotel guests, servants, valets—remained disinterested and silent. But the disaster, and his part in it, changed all that. Since then he could feel the burning heat of the lamp, the hush of interest, the magnified attention, the crowds gathering to view and confer, and has never quite shaken himself free of it.

Staring through the glass now at the attendant's left shoulder and twitching gloved hands, the whole exercise seems like hopeless bravado, and so clearly not what Evelyn wanted. Never has he seen such mortification on his daughter's face as when he unsuccessfully tried to bluff his intentions.

"I find I have to rush into the lobby for an errand, my dear."

"No, Father," she said.

"It's all right, really. Everything will be all right."

He remembers the last time he spoke that promise, a burning, foolish one, on a freezing deck minutes after receiving news that the ship would founder. It seemed a sensible thing to say at the time, as belief in safety eased the passengers into the lifeboats far more efficiently than signs of danger that elicited questions and a general agitation. Everything, of course, was not all right. He knew the gash under the waterline ran along at least four watertight compartments and he knew, without Andrews' confirmation, what that meant.

A party of two women and one man strolls by the

phones. One of the women glances in his direction and he finds himself hunching and turning, like Grimsden in the adjacent box, a pose he would likely use if he were talking to someone. The earpiece is hot against his lobe and the flex slaps gently to the rhythm of his pulse against his palm. He notices the fabric covering the wire becomes damper with sweat each time it touches upon his skin. The subterfuge infuriates him, makes everything seem urgent, and when he hears the creak of Grimsden's opening door, he drops the earpiece and steps outside.

Ismay is close enough to feel Grimsden's body heat as the unsuspecting man places a piece of paper in his wallet and slides the wallet into the inner lining of his jacket pocket. It's a moment until he looks up, startled, brown eyes staring into Ismay's face. The physical closeness is too awkward. Ismay shuffles slightly backwards but delivers the challenge quickly.

"I want a word with you, Grimsden."

Grimsden's face changes, his eyebrows raising. Understanding, a hint of dark humour perhaps, comes into his expression.

"Your wife has been staring at us through dinner." The same party that passed the phones now returns in the opposite direction. The young woman who glanced at him then, does so again now. The gentle conversation of the party ceases altogether. Ismay realizes his words may have carried. "She has quite upset my daughter."

"When it comes to that, Mr. Ismay, your daughter may have caused us some problems with digestion too. And it was not a cheap meal."

"Is that all you've got to say?"

The group of three has passed now, silently, going toward the elevators leading to the rooms and suites. They begin to murmur, and the other lady takes a swift backward glance. The phone attendant stands by the farthest door. He looks straight ahead like a soldier, but his expression is worried.

"What would you have me say? It's an argument between the womenfolk. Why don't you let them sort it out?"

The logic of it hits Ismay like a wall, but he knows logic can't satisfy him. Evelyn can't sort it out, and he doesn't want her to try. If there is a cause for Mrs. Grimsden's insulting behaviour, it is he. And he can't argue with Mrs. Grimsden, so he must do the next best thing. He must challenge her husband.

"I think you and I should sort it out."

Grimsden smiles. Joviality has an odd effect upon his bulldog appearance, bringing his jowly cheeks up several inches, transforming him into an unlikely Father Christmas.

"It's been some considerable time since I've received such an offer. Will it be fisticuffs in the street or should we look into the cost of booking the Albert Hall and give everyone a laugh?"

"I'm sorry you should find it so amusing." Ismay finds his eyes watering, is ashamed of how this must look, but feels he may explode with the impotence of his fury. "But my family have heard me called coward once too often, and you are responsible for your wife whether you realize it or not."

Grimsden sighs. "Mr. Ismay, unless you are talking about the processes of law, libel and so forth, Agnes is responsible for Agnes, I am responsible for me, and you are responsible for you."

Ismay finds himself squaring up, shoulder sinews tightening. Improbable and undignified as he knows it will be, he is on the brink, eyes skimming Grimsden's bloated left ear with its tuft of brown hair, the pitted flesh of his nose for the likely landfall of a first blow. But he needs the trigger word—*coward*—and Grimsden will persist in skirting it. "For the record, Mr. Ismay, I've no reason to doubt your personal courage. No, I know how newspapers and gossip work. But what did you think was going to happen when you were saved?"

The phone attendant, who had been watching with growing alarm, is distracted by an elderly man asking directions. Ismay feels he is at a multiple-lane crossroads, baffled by Grimsden's contradictions, harried by the constricts of time and opportunity. "You've had the rewards, Mr. Ismay. First class all the way, birth on upwards. Why should you avoid paying the price?"

"What is this?" Ismay says with a laugh. Only a trace of spittle sparking under the light differentiates his tone from pure, detached scorn. But his body does relax. This is all he has been fighting for the last thirteen years, he thinks: a brazen, primitive absence of logic. "I've had it good. I've attracted envy. So now I must pay. Is that it?"

"I dare say that's what it boils down to, Mr. Ismay." Grimsden tucks the fingertips of his right hand into his waistcoat pocket. "You know your history, no doubt, but I'm not talking about the classics—Greek and whatnot—but plain, ordinary English history. The heir to a throne, you'll remember, is a target for assassination from the moment he can crawl. All his rivals need is a cause, just or otherwise. That's all your rivals needed too, and you gave it to them."

"And how about you, Mr. Grimsden?" Ismay finds himself trembling. Now he will turn the tables. Now he'll break a hole through Grimsden's self-satisfied air and make him strike first. "Did you also not have fortune in your own career? Your marriage, for instance?"

"My marriage?" Grimsden tilts his head, brown eyes shining.

"She's the heiress of a shipbuilding company, too, I gather. What does that make you?"

Ismay senses he's just stepped into the dark. This is what Mrs. Grimsden said, isn't it? He traces urgently through thirteen-year-old snatches of conversation. Her father was a shipbuilder in Halifax, Nova Scotia. He is sure he heard so much, either from the Grimsdens themselves or from the Foresters who provided the introduction, although the name of the company eludes him.

"Oh, my father-in-law built ships all right, Mr. Ismay," he says now, folding his arms over his chest. "And he was much more of a shipbuilder in a practical sense than you or your celebrated father. Between you and me now, as Agnes never says a word to a living soul. But my father-in-law was a ship's carpenter."

Ismay moves backwards, suspecting a trick, *hoping* for evidence of a trick. But another look at Grimsden's indomitable expression and the agitation in his nerves dissolves to defeat.

"When I met Agnes, Mr. Ismay, she was seventeen years old, penniless, in service to a Manchester family much like your own, business owners for generations." He hums in consideration, clearly enjoying Ismay's discomfort. "I was an employee somewhat overwhelmed to be invited to their party. All the silk, the gold, the genuine pearls, made me restless." He scratches a furry earlobe at the memory. "But you wouldn't know about that. Naturally I found myself gravitating to the servants, especially the young redhead with the slightly haughty manner—yes; she had it then—from Nova Scotia. I liked the ring of that name, New Scotland. 'Better than the old one,' it seemed to say, and I myself was moving into new territory."

He holds up a finger as if to flag a point in danger of escaping. "But she was poor, Mr. Ismay, not a businessman's daughter at all, but a serf like me, determined to improve her lot in life. You see, I imagine that, whether or not she knows it herself, her dislike of you—which I will not, by the way, trouble to deny—has nothing to do with 'women and children first.' No. In some dim corner of my wife's mind she knows that had we *not* prospered as we did, had she boarded the *Titanic* in steerage class, as she would have been obliged to do, my wife and her daughter would have shared the fate of the rest of her class and accompanied your fine vessel in its long and freezing journey to the bottom of the ocean."

The phone attendant, relieved now, glances at them as he opens the door for a lady in a feather hat. Grimsden stares at Ismay for a moment. He turns his wrist inwards to glance at his watch. "Now, Mr. Ismay, if there is nothing more, I shall return to my table. Well . . ." With a final shrug, Grimsden departs, leaving in his wake the scent of sweet tobacco and wine.

Ismay finds he's unable even to turn toward the dining room for fear of the life within—the shimmering dresses, the rising smoke, and the beating fans. He hears a splash somewhere close, off to his right, a sound so resonant, so fully embodied and real, he's surprised to see not a length of oar half submerged in rippling dark waters, but rather the richly patterned red Persian carpet. There's no explanation for the noise, no jugs of water on trays, just the Ritz lobby, the phone attendant, looking straight ahead, with white-gloved hands at his sides.

Ismay thinks of the questions at the enquiry about why he had his back to the sinking ship. He'd had to explain he was at the oars, pulling, and that his back was turned not from choice. He wasn't in charge of the lifeboat. It was the truth too. But he wonders if it could have been any other way. If a clear-sighted vision had accompanied the thunderous groans of buckling metal, the crashes of boilers and engines slamming through bulkheads, and worst of all, the human sounds—the endless, agonizing wailing—he wonders whether he would have been able to see again. Would the lush rolling hills of his chosen retreat in Ireland, the face of his wife or his children have become forever superimposed with the images of destruction—his ship upended in the water, its lights still burning, great clusters of people like ants clinging to the stern, some dropping, bouncing against the hull on the way to certain death? It seems more than a lucky chance now that he should have been facing the other way.

As he turns to go back into the dining room at last, he promises himself it will be his last time here, the last time in London or in any English city, his last appearance among the crowds. He feels the tramp of the Connemara turf beneath his feet, damp but solid enough, more firm than anything under the souls who perished thirteen

Aprils ago. Oblivion wants him and the desire is mutual. He has outlived his time.

HE SMILES AT EVELYN as he sits, notes the battle of emotion there—worry, relief, and urgent need to know—and feels the profound peace of a man who knows a war to be finally over, and the only chore remaining to be the announcement of the fact. The waiter slides dessert plates before Evelyn, then before Ismay.

"Most efficient, thank you," he says. The waiter's face twitches and he hurries off.

"Father." Evelyn leans toward him. "What happened?"

"What happened?" Ismay echoes, raising his dessert fork. "About fifteen hundred people died on one of my steamships in 1912."

Evelyn stares, open-mouthed. She seems suddenly so young, this daughter of his, in her fashionable loose-fitting dress, with the pink in her cheeks. He's become used to thinking of her as a wise old woman in the body of a girl, and wonders whether it's because he's always felt so shielded, so taken care of, in her presence. It seems an injustice to her now. She is indeed as young as she looks.

Evelyn hesitates, lifts her own fork, and stops again.

"Father, what do you mean?"

Her eyes are intent upon him, aware that there *is* a meaning, that this is not merely the prelude to a nervous breakdown.

"I mean, my dear, that the only thing that should ever have mattered is the disaster and what caused it." He taps with the side of his fork on the hard sugar coating of his crème brûlée.

"Isn't that the problem, Father? People seemed to think that *you* caused it, and we have to put them right."

"It was my ship, Evelyn. There were design flaws and there were not enough lifeboats. Someone has to take the blame."

Despite the calmness in his voice, he sees disquiet in her eyes. He lays his fork down.

"Evelyn, there comes a time in everyone's life when after years of building, of pursuing some goal or other, one simply has to say: enough; I've done my part for good or ill. I was at that point in 1912, ready to retire, to move gracefully off into the file drawers of the White Star Line. But the *Titanic* prevented me. It couldn't be the last word, this appalling disaster, this unthinkable loss of life, the shame of it all."

"Yet you did resign within a few months."

A cloud seems to pass over Evelyn, the shadow of a waiter perhaps. Ismay wonders if she's afraid his memory is going.

"I physically left the workplace, yes."

"And against the wishes of your colleagues," she prompts quickly.

"Against the wishes of *some* of them, yes. They understood me, just as you do."

A flicker of gratitude comes into Evelyn's eyes.

"But I never left the deck of the *Titanic*. And why should I? Others weren't allowed to."

Her lip trembles and he sees her wrestle with something.

"You blame yourself, Father." She nudges forward in her chair, a coil of energy about to be released, and he can feel it coming, the same arguments against his guilt. He knows them all by rote. He took no one's place in the lifeboat. It would have been a pointless act of self-sacrifice. He hadn't influenced the captain on that night, had no say at all in navigation. He holds up his hand to stop her, hushing her like a child.

"And who else is there to blame?" he asks quietly. "Fifteen hundred people, Evelyn. Some of them never even made it to the boat decks until the lifeboats had all gone—steerage people."

Evelyn catches his eye, then looks down and presses the base of her glass to the tablecloth as though they are on a dining car of a train and she is preventing the motion of the tracks from making it spill. "Thomas Andrews designed the ship, Father."

"And who hired and directed Thomas Andrews?"

She looks up at him again, eyes damp.

"No more arguing," he says, "no more stating of my case, either to myself or to others. You freed me of it all tonight, Evelyn. You showed me again how futile it was to go through it over and over, to try and face out your accuser. After tonight I shall finally leave the *Titanic*."

"Leave?" A hint of alarm sparks in her eyes.

"Nothing drastic." He picks up his glass and holds it toward her. "Tomorrow, I return to Liverpool to pick up your mother and thence to Ireland, where I shall live the life of a country squire."

Evelyn sighs and he can feel the warm breath of her relief.

"From now on you'll have to visit me, you and your Basil. He will have to do the building from now on."

She gives him a shy smile. He's well aware that Evelyn tries to rouse him by suggesting how similar her intended is, in character, to himself. Ismay often sidesteps the intended compliment as Basil is a decorated war hero and the contrast is too painful, the flattery too undeserved. This reciprocation will, he hopes, reassure her.

"I'm glad we came here tonight, Evelyn," he tells her, raising the fork to his mouth.

He sees sadness behind her smile, as well as acceptance, and a quiet breeze moves over them, swaying the heavy leaves of the palm.

chapter thirteen

MIRANDA'S BEEN TRYING TO fathom things since her father returned. But the conversation, mainly between Graham and Mother and about the benefits of different areas of London, keeps distracting her. She has to keep an eye on her fiancé to prevent Mother from breaking through his wall. Graham seems dithery now, and tired, and Mother's probing is all the more intense. The only sign that anything happened at all outside the dining room is Father's mildly fed-up sigh as he resumed his seat, a quick look at the table and a tetchy glance at his watch.

Mr. Ismay returned a few moments later and, despite the expression on Evelyn's face when her father left, he seems relaxed enough. The conversation she's spied through the palm seemed a little intense, perhaps, but calm. It's a strange feeling. For thirteen years she's believed that her actions may well have caused untold grief and fury. The feeling swelled to a dizzying height tonight but has collapsed into this: two men who seem hardly interested at all. That she should experience it as an anticlimax causes real disquiet. Is this what she wanted, and still wants now, to be noticed, hated, and despised? It brings her back to her ten-year-old self sitting alone in the dimness of her father's study, surrounded by the fragrance of embossed leather and bonded paper, scratching hateful lines with her new fountain pen.

Mother breaks through the memory, her voice rising in triumph.

"Belgravia! Not Chelsea! Oh, Miranda, I'm so glad."

"What?" The word comes out in a gasp. She fires a look at Graham whose neck is suddenly pink with embarrassment.

"My dear, the cat's out of the bag! Graham has been telling me your plans."

She stares at her mother. Defeat, she is beginning to realize, was almost inevitable but she's amazed at Mother's powers of resilience, her easy recovery. The tiredness has gone from her eyes, replaced by the malicious life and artificial poise that always seem to mark family celebrations.

"Yes, you got it out of me, Mrs. G., you're far too clever," says Graham nervously, eyes darting toward Miranda.

Miranda knows it shouldn't really matter whether

Mother knows where they plan to live, and that she would find out anyway in time. But her not knowing gave Miranda a sense of security, albeit a symbolic one. Graham's leak of the information has likely given Mother the go-ahead to descend upon everything, not only wedding preparations, but the precise house as well. She will surely pressure them both to buy a larger place than is financially comfortable. She will advise about staff, remind them both how she abhors the modern fad for doing without. She will give her views upon the schooling of their future children. In that word "Belgravia" she has achieved the first victory, always the hardest to win. Now the precedent for Graham crumbling has been set, the barriers that keep Miranda from being too much like her mother will fall, one after the other, until one day in twenty or thirty years' time, Mother's face will gaze back at her from her mirror.

Graham continues to look desperate but Miranda is drifting away into defeat, just as Mother was a few minutes ago, sinking back into the recollection of Father's study, of coming to give him his tobacco, and feeling his great meaty arms pull her onto his knee as he did every once in a while when the mood took him, usually after a long day's work, some unexpected good news. She remembers laughing along with him, being told to "run along now."

* * *

"COME TO THE PARK with us," Miranda says, flushed with the moment.

"I'll have to write a letter," he says shaking his head, filling his pipe, "an important letter, Miranda."

"Can't you do it later?" she insists.

"Business first, pleasure later." His low voice, vibrating through the furniture, seems to embody the spirit of an adult world that is beyond understanding, a world of pipes, tobacco, embossed leather, urgent letters and no parks, no swings, no outside at all. But the comfort it gives Miranda is profound, a return to cast-iron certainty after the strangeness of the *Titanic*, New York, and Mr. Johnston. She can almost forget there ever was such a man, that the summer in New York was merely part of an eerie dream from which she has now awakened.

Miranda backs off but holds onto the doorknob. She thinks about trying again. Father strikes his match and sets it into the bowl of his pipe, puffing and pulling. "A friend of your mother, Mr. Johnston in fact, has, through contacts, helped to get us a very important deal with a company in the United States. And I should not wait a moment before thanking him properly. Run along now!"

Miranda feels a blight in the air as her short legs try to keep up with Mother, watching from a yard's distance the breeze shivering through her mother's stole. The pavement is still slippery underfoot from the morning's rain, and a wasp, lazy in the cooling air but persistent, buzzes around her head. Early fallen leaves scattered around in dry patches seem to whisper *Mr. Johnston, Mr. Johnston,* and Miranda tries to remember the conversation in the museum. She looks up at her mother, wondering how to dip once again into those mysteries, but Mother has that faraway look, the smile she reserves for stories of heroism, for their evocations in art and poetry. *Selflessness and sacrifice are true measures of nobility*—the phrase resurfaces, hauling many tangled strands of confusion. She said at the time that Father needed help but didn't know how to ask for it. She also talked about discretion. And here is her father, her kindly but fearless father, reduced to blind, unknowing servility to Mr. Johnston at whom he, by rights, should be outraged.

The wasp buzzes around her again, clumsily prods her forehead close to her hairline. She almost wishes it would sting. Like a dark, underground stream, the vaguest, most terrifying feeling meanders through her: something has gone terribly wrong. When that great steamship foundered, it took the ordinary world, and all that is safe and reliable, with it. Now she views the world through a distorting mirror. Heroism has turned to treachery. Brave strong men, like her father, have become obsequious.

The park comes into view and Mother takes her hand. A rush of pity and regret floods Miranda. She looks up at this elegant woman with her high cheekbones and her proud air and knows she didn't mean to betray Father. It's all a terrible mistake. The wasp touches down on her wrist then flies off as Mother and she stand upon the curb, waiting for a motor car to pass. As she remembers the collage she had made of the newspaper article, a new emotion begins to rumble within Miranda; it's a stark and fire-spitting feeling, and she no longer pities the Ismay girls. She's on her mother's side, this time, fending off the snakes. Something loosed evil upon the world that spring, and it wasn't Mother. Leaves skitter along the road and the name they whisper changes from *Johnston* to *Ismay* as they cross to the rolling trees and the dappled sunlight of the park.

The worst kind of villain is one who makes good people act against their own judgment. It was Ismay's ship; Ismay, whom her father seemed to look up to in that strange, silent way of his; Ismay who shattered Mother's notions of good and evil; and Ismay who should be made to pay for it all. She thinks of her father's study, his black leather-bound address book, his stamps, and with a small flutter in her chest, sets her plan in motion.

MIRANDA SEES SOMETHING BEYOND the palm, and this time there is a conclusive air about the movement. Mr. Ismay comes around the table and puts a thin shawl around his daughter's shoulders. Evelyn stands and straightaway turns to leave, but Mr. Ismay waits for a moment and looks in Miranda's direction.

She's too numbed to notice properly at first; the illusion has returned that she's at the theatre, and therefore beyond being seen. But he holds her gaze until she glances away, then back again. Her face gives a slight twitch of apology. While she has no idea what this expression might look like, something about the way Mr. Ismay meets her gaze once again seems to acknowledge this. He turns and follows his daughter.

Miranda is left alone with Father, Graham, and Mother. The talk now is of the best curtains and light fittings, about Harrods, and Fortnum and Mason's, and the horrors of modern department stores with their low prices but dubious goods. Miranda thinks of breaking in but knows it's far too late. Mother's eyes are lively, reflecting the chandeliers now, basking in the gentle breeze. This time, Miranda realizes, it is curiosity rather than annoyance that was behind her instinct to interrupt. She's too defeated to try to rebuild the defensive wall.

There have never been any relatives on Mother's side, or any long-term friends who might have known her in childhood, who might have shed light on her extraordinary perseverance when it comes to upholding all that is correct in taste and conduct. Yet it has been quite relentless, and she can right herself in minutes and steam ahead as she has done tonight after any argument or unpleasantness. Even her breach of the basic vows of fidelity—the veiled threat of discovery tonight—can't bow her indomitable spirit. It's possible Father has remained ignorant about it all these years—although he does manifest a rather pointed dislike of his wife at times, which makes Miranda wonder—but Mother herself has always seemed quite untroubled by the subject of Mr. Johnston, even laughs in a rather shrill and overly public manner at pleasantries still written on Christmas cards, which are addressed, rather revealingly, only to Mother.

Somehow the notion of greater advancement, her family's place in the social sphere, must, for Mother, transcend any parochial objections. The values are as baffling as they are distorted, but the sheer stoicism of it all astonishes Miranda. In recent years, Miranda has seen her mother as something grand, powerful yet flawed; one of the great steamships of the past transformed and personified. But suddenly she seems altogether harsher, more enduring, and at heart, chillingly cold.

Since she became an adult, capable of arguing, Miranda has merely taken the opposite view as a reaction and has never learned a thing about what lies inside her mother. She remembers the heated discussions of late— *The world is changing, Mother. Classes are merging. The wealthy are being taxed. And most of them give in with a grumble or two and admit it. Even if you are close to the top of the sinking pyramid, you must realize it's disappearing—* and realizes her words were as inert as printed letters on a page. What was there in any of it to provoke a reaction? Where was the engagement? Now, for the first time, as she watches the inexhaustible stars in Mother's eyes, the glint of light upon the gold earring chains, the dark pools of onyx sewn into her mint green dress, she sees her mother as a genuine mystery. She wonders what it might be like to ask a simple, open-ended question of the kind she complains her fiancé avoids. Such a question, calculated for greatest surprise, gathers on her lips: *Mother, why is any of this important?*

A pause opens up and Miranda is within a whisker of speaking.

"Graham," Mother announces, "you must get Miranda to hire a lady's maid."

Miranda gulps down the question, bites her lip.

Mother glides on, sparkling into the night, and the moment passes.

acknowledgements

I would like to thank Garry Cranford and Jerry Cranford for their enthusiasm for this novel and everyone at Flanker Press, including publicist Laura Cameron, for their attention to this book. For this story I was particularly lucky with editors and would like to thank Marnie Parsons for her expert care and attention to detail, and Annamarie Beckel for her wise and subtle judgment. As always, I would like to thank Maura, my wonderful wife and partner, and my joyful little daughter, Jemma.

PAUL BUTLER is the author of several critically acclaimed novels, including *Cupids, Hero, 1892, NaGeira, Easton's Gold, Easton,* and *Stoker's Shadow*. His work has appeared on the judges' lists for Canada Reads and the Relit Longlist for three consecutive years, and he was a winner in the Government of Newfoundland and Labrador Arts and Letters Awards four times between 2003 and 2008, when he retired from the competition to be literary representative, and then chair, of the Arts and Letters Committee. A graduate of Norman Jewison's Canadian Film Centre, Butler has written for the *Globe and Mail, The Beaver, Books in Canada, Atlantic Books Today,* and *Canadian Geographic*, and has also contributed to CBC Radio, local and national. He lives in St. John's. His website is www.paulbutlernovelist.com.

Easton's Gold

". . . Butler builds solid suspense and healthy narrative momentum through a focus on fundamentals: efficient storytelling, keen attention to characterization and fealty to the mysteries of the past and their influence on the present . . . a compelling novel which often surprises and satisfies." — THE GLOBE AND MAIL

"Butler is an invigorating writer, keeping the reader in suspense, but moving the story along at an exhilarating pace. . . . And finally, Butler is a fine stylist, one who knows how to provide apt images that vivify thought and action." — CANADIAN BOOK REVIEW ANNUAL

"*Easton's Gold* and its predecessor [*Easton*] are about as different as it's possible for two novels featuring the same character to be. They're both excellent, but in very different ways." — THE CHRONICLE HERALD

Cupids

"Butler does a good job of bringing out that 'unstated drama' in *Cupids* . . . [providing] enough detail to give you a sense of life in the 1600s. . . . Another of his strengths as a writer is an ability to quickly create a picture of a character, one that stays with you."
THE CHRONICLE HERALD

Easton

"The story is fast-paced, action-packed, and replete with horrific details, frequent tests of will, a somewhat improbable love match, and a satisfying denouement."
CANADIAN BOOK REVIEW ANNUAL

"[*Easton*] is exceptionally well-written. . . . Throughout the novel, the atmosphere of threatening danger that permeates the story will hold the reader spellbound until the end." — THE TELEGRAM

1892

"[*1892*] is a page turner that will be enjoyed as romance, historical fiction and a chilling gothic tale."
ATLANTIC BOOKS TODAY

"[Paul Butler's] writing is lyrical and compelling."
THE SUDBURY STAR

"Beautifully written . . ."
BOOK-A-RAMA

"[Paul Butler's] descriptions of how people find themselves in old St. John's are persuasive and compelling."
RESOURCE LINKS